PENGUIN BOOKS

GRAYS HARBOR

Robert A. Weinstein was formerly Graphics Editor of the *American West Magazine* and Art Director of the *Quarterly of the California Historical Society*, successfully pioneering the photo-essay in both publications. Well known as a consultant in maritime history and in the photographic history of the United States, he specializes in frontier photography and recently published a major work in the field, *Collection, Care and Use of Historical Photographs*. He is also coauthor of *Dwellers at the Source: The Southwest Indian Photographs of Adam Clark Vroman;* and he wrote the texts for *The West: An American Experience* and *The Taming of the West*. Among positions he currently holds are those of Research Associate in Western History at the Natural History Museum of Los Angeles County, Research Associate in Pacific Coast Maritime History for the Bernice P. Bishop Museum in Honolulu, and Chairman of the History and Research Committee of the Maritime Museum Association of San Diego, which owns the restored sailing vessel *Star of India*. Articles and reviews by him frequently appear in popular, professional, and scholarly periodicals.

1885-1913 Grays

Robert A. Weinstein

Harbor

Penguin Books

Penguin Books Ltd, Harmondsworth,
Middlesex, England
Penguin Books, 625 Madison Avenue,
New York, New York 10022, U.S.A.
Penguin Books Australia Ltd, Ringwood,
Victoria, Australia
Penguin Books Canada Limited, 2801 John Street,
Markham, Ontario, Canada L3R 1B4
Penguin Books (N.Z.) Ltd, 182–190 Wairau Road,
Auckland 10, New Zealand

First published in the United States of America
in simultaneous hardcover and paperback editions
by The Viking Press and Penguin Books 1978

LIBRARY OF CONGRESS CATALOGING IN PUBLICATION DATA
Weinstein, Robert A.
    Grays Harbor, 1885–1913.
    1. Grays Harbor, Wash.—History. I. Title.
F899.G73w44   979.7'95'04   77-17040
ISBN 0 14 00.4890 1

Printed in the United States of America by
The Murray Printing Company,
Westford, Massachusetts
Set in Memphis Light and Memphis Medium

ACKNOWLEDGMENTS

This book required help, and it was given generously by many individuals. These persons, many of them good friends, were of invaluable assistance, raising and answering questions, verifying inquiries, and providing identification for many of the photographs.

Harry and Matilda Dring, Aberdeen residents in their youth, volunteered information and critical opinion; their open-handed contributions could not have been exceeded. Earle Connette, Head of the Manuscript-Archives Division of the Washington State University Library which owns the Pratsch collection, and his assistant Terry Abraham made the negatives available for this book and shared with me their own careful work, suggesting additional sources for information. Norman Nelson, photographer for the Library at W.S.U., made the handsome prints reproduced herein from the original glass negatives.

Robert D. Monroe, Special Collections Librarian at the University of Washington Library, offered good advice and information and faithfully produced readable Xerox copies of necessary documents.

Special appreciation is owed to Fred Pratsch, who throughout his eighty-year life never wavered in his determination to see his father's work preserved and used. Although Ed Van Syckle, Grays Harbor newspaperman and the dean of local historians, generously provided the backbone of knowledge I needed to write this book, he bears no responsibility for any errors or omissions; they are mine alone.

To my wife, Vivian, and son, David, who offered informed counsel, reinforcing sympathy, and encouragement, my deepest thanks.

R.W.

This book is gratefully dedicated
to Earle Connette.
He knew the first time he saw these
photographs that they needed to be saved,
and he saw to it that they were.

Contents

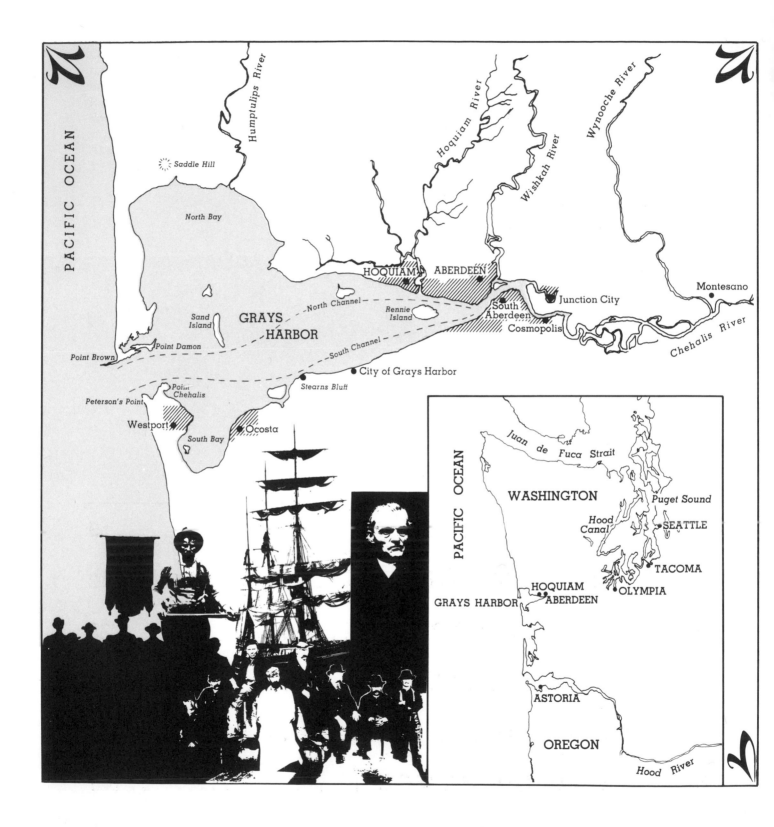

PACIFIC OCEAN

Humptulips River

Hoquiam River

Wishkah River

Wynooche River

☼ *Saddle Hill*

North Bay

HOQUIAM ABERDEEN

Montesano

Sand Island

GRAYS HARBOR

North Channel

Rennie Island

South
Aberdeen

Junction City

Cosmopolis

Chehalis River

Point Damon

South Channel

Point Brown

City of Grays Harbor

Point Chehalis

Stearns Bluff

Peterson's Point

Westport

South Bay

Ocosta

Juan de Fuca Strait

PACIFIC OCEAN

WASHINGTON

Puget Sound

Hood Canal

SEATTLE

TACOMA

HOQUIAM

OLYMPIA

GRAYS HARBOR

ABERDEEN

ASTORIA

OREGON

Hood River

Introduction

Although no other graphic image can rival a photograph for credibility, and sometimes for penetrating and moving eloquence, photographs even at their best are limited witnesses with restricted vision. They cannot show us *everything* one wishes to know of people, places, and events. Usually they reveal what was important to the photographer and little else. Still, even though each experience, each singular image, is a statement of no more than the instant of time it encompasses, a photograph can disclose information that many viewers might overlook with the naked eye, or it can show them things they might prefer not to see at all.

The photographs of Grays Harbor reproduced in this book are often this type of visual document. Taken by four local photographers, they form a fragmented but magnificent view of a brief period in the life of the harbor's infant communities. In these photographs we can share the pride of every man, woman, and child in those harbor towns whose brief moments of immortality are transfixed in these images. We might even see them with increased understanding as they parade through these pages, the loggers, sailors, farmers, businessmen, and prostitutes of Grays Harbor's yesterdays. These are eloquent images, many of them offering reminders of other ways of living, of life styles quite common among our forebears not too long ago in the United States.

Most of the photographs were taken by Charles R. Pratsch of Aberdeen. A few were made by Colin S. McKenzie, a young logger whom Pratsch introduced to photography. Jesse O. Stearns, a young Hoquiam banker, took some of them, and the rest are by one or more photographers not yet identified.

There is little doubt that these photographs were widely seen and admired at Grays Harbor. Although Pratsch was in business as a photographer in Aberdeen, there is no evidence that he sold many of his photographs. His negatives were little used after 1913, and for many years until his death in 1937 they lay hidden away in a closet of the Pratsch studio in Aberdeen. After his passing the collection went to his youngest son, Fred V. Pratsch, who cherished the inheritance, recognizing its documentary value from the first. As he grew older he exercised his own talent for painting, making copies of the photographs on canvas in oils. He rarely refused requests to exhibit both the paintings and the hand-colored slides he made from the photographs at public gatherings in Aberdeen and Hoquiam. These showings in Grays Harbor communities attracted interest in and new appreciation for the photographs, recognition which Fred Pratsch believed his father's work richly deserved. Such approval strengthened his determination to preserve his father's legacy. He knew he would never be able to provide the trained archival care the negatives required; he could not even offer them a secure home for the future.

I first became aware of the Pratsch collection through the advice of several friends who had seen it and recognized its value as an unusual visual record of Pacific Coast maritime history. I tried several times unsuccessfully to purchase it from Fred Pratsch for the San Francisco Maritime Museum. Other institutions made unacceptable offers to buy the negatives at bargain rates or asked him to donate them as a tax-free gift. Each of these requests was rejected, as well as similar ones from out-of-state institutions. Fred Pratsch had always insisted that the negatives remain in Washington, where they had the greatest meaning. On this point he was adamant and unmoving.

He gave up his teamster business in Aberdeen, moving his family to the south shore beaches near Westport where he undertook a new business venture, commercial fishing. This is a risky and uncertain way of making a living at best, and his modest home at Bay City was a symbol of his marginal successes. In the new home, where storage facilities were severely limited, some neglect of the precious photographic plates was unavoidable. For long periods of time the negatives in their original cardboard containers were piled in wooden shotgun-shell boxes and then simply stacked alongside the unsheathed interior walls. They could not avoid becoming victims of rain, heat, humid spells, and salt sea air . . . each in a different way seriously damaging to photographs. It is a small miracle that so few of the surviving images have deteriorated so little.

Fred Pratsch became increasingly aware of the urgent need to dispose of the negatives responsibly. Only his steady resolve to see the collection properly secured has made it available today. His firm stewardship and Earle Connette's quick recognition of the value of the negatives turned the trick at the right time.

Mr. Connette, then Chief of the Manuscript-Archives Division of the Washington State University Library, successfully offered Fred Pratsch the proper price and the responsible home he had hoped to find for the collection. He was convinced that the negatives and prints would be well taken care of in the University Library at Pullman, Washington, and their availability for public use guaranteed. The sale and transfer of the materials to the University Library was completed in July 1971.

Under Mr. Connette's direction the work needed to preserve the collection has already been carried out. The negatives have been cleaned, rejacketed, and catalogued, carefully printed by W. S. U. photographer Norman Nelson, and safely stored in metal cabinets under archival conditions. The photographs have begun to be publicized and the value of the collection is becoming better known. Research continues, adding new information about the life and times at Grays Harbor portrayed in the photographs. They remain eloquent evidence of Charles Robert Pratsch's sympathetic vision. These images of the Grays Harbor he knew so well, his legacy, are secure at last.

It is a stroke of good fortune that the Pratsch photographs of Grays Harbor can still be seen, studied, and enjoyed. Far too many equally worthy nineteenth-century images are buried in the collections of now-dead photographers, particularly those whose life's work was centered in similar small towns and villages. They often lie in obscurity, forgotten and useless. Such priceless images of our history await discovery and use, their ability to serve, inform, and teach not yet finished. When will they once again see the light of day?

Robert A. Weinstein
1978

Grays Harbor Country 1885-1913

It may have been no more than a spasm of nature, a tremor of the forming earth's crust, that first created Grays Harbor. Melting snows rushing off the Sierra's western flanks helped deepen the harbor. Whatever the truth of its geological history, it is one of a thousand bays, coves, and inlets, sea havens of every description, that indent the fifteen-hundred-mile-long Pacific coastline of the United States.

That coast is brutal for seafarers. Unlike the Atlantic Coast, over ninety per cent of the Pacific Coast is rough, heavily wooded terrain with rockbound cliffs, deep water close to the shore, and visible and hidden reefs that extend seaward for miles. Here are dense fogs, contrary currents, and murderous sand bars blocking the mouths of most useful rivers. Navigators and seamen of past centuries learned to approach landfalls on this coast with caution and apprehension.

As the narrowing Chehalis River twisted upstream, eastward, Aberdeen on its north bank was finally united with South Aberdeen and Cosmopolis on its south shore in 1907 when the A. J. West bridge shown here was completed. Its center span was a wooden swing bridge to permit the river traffic passage upstream. The bridge honored Aberdeen's pioneer lumberman, A. J. West, whose founding mill in 1885 was located close to this location where the Wishkah meets the Chehalis.

From his vantage on the Isthmus of Panama in 1513, Balboa thought the Pacific Ocean peaceful and so named it. By and large it is a misnomer on North American shores, where the names given by sailors to landmarks on the Pacific Coast have a chilling appropriateness: Cape Disappointment, Cape Flattery, False Bay, Cape Foulweather, Cape Shoalwater, Point Defiance, Point Misery, and Destruction Island. Explicitness has always ruled the choosing of such names by exploring seafarers. Captain James Cook, a laconic Yorkshireman, must have been driven to great lengths of endurance to choose names like Disappointment, Foulweather, Flattery, and Misery.

Europeans began the exploration of the Northwest coast in the sixteenth century. James Cook, Sir Francis Drake, LaPérouse, George Vancouver, and scores of others left their names upon the land. In this lot it is a young Rhode Islander, an unassuming shipmaster named Robert Gray, a former officer in the Continental Navy, who interests us most. On August 9, 1790, as Master of the American ship *Columbia Rediviva,* he reentered Boston Harbor after an absence of three years; it was the first ship to carry an American flag around the world. Captain Gray hurried to report to Governor John Hancock on the opening of the Northwest fur trade, the successful beginning of an endeavor that opened the door of the legendary China trade for Boston merchants.

It is not this single accomplishment of Robert Gray that compels our interest, nor even his discovery and entrance into the mouth of the river he called Columbia, claiming it for the infant country he represented. Rather, it is that, on the second voyage of the same Boston ship on May 7, 1792, Robert Gray discovered another river entrance north of the mighty Columbia River, the second largest bay between Cape Disappointment and Cape Flattery. He named it Bulfinch's Harbor, after Charles Bulfinch, one of the principal owners of his vessel. In October of the same year a certain young Whidbey, a lieutenant in Vancouver's storeship, *Daedelus,* was sent with crews in small boats to explore and survey Bulfinch's Harbor. He renamed it Grays Harbor in just tribute to its discoverer.

Grays Harbor is at once both beautiful and awesome. Its color scheme was then, and is yet, gray and green. Its chief green glories are mammoth trees—fir, spruce, hemlock, and cedar that line the land horizon in all directions. Its gray miseries are rain-heavy clouds hanging in leaden skies. It is wet and dank there, the ground is soggy, and everywhere the forest drips. Winters are fierce, the rain falling endlessly and freezing quickly. Summers and springs are temperate but even wetter. The rainfall in Grays Harbor, over a hundred inches each year, defies belief. But there is pure air in abundance, and the skies are a visual delight when not filled with rain. The bay and the ocean offer their own special beauty as often as one cares to look for it.

This isolated, sea-fronted wilderness, rich in lumber and teeming with fish, was destined to become a sawmilling center in southwestern Washington, a major lumber supplier for the busy, growing outside world, a seaport of long-remembered fame, a sailor's sinful heaven-on-earth lurid enough to rival San Francisco's Barbary Coast, and finally a center of shipbuilding, innovative in design and method, on the Pacific Coast.

Grays Harbor, that wet, insect-ridden confluence of five rivers, triggered men's imagination for a hundred years. Dreamers came and lived on big dreams. A few dreams were realized, most were not. Fortunes were planned, and a few were made and kept; most were not. Railroads were planned that never arrived, and great harbor constructions were envisioned that were never built. The record of the vigorous pioneers who migrated into the Grays Harbor country is a story of endurance, courage, good will, and an unbelievable amount of hard labor. These pioneers were plain people, not monuments of goodness or pillars of simple virtue; they were complex, diverse, capricious, and as unpredictable as any other human beings. They cleared the land, felled trees, created sawmills, and built villages from their own cut lumber. They fished and bridged the rivers, built ships, and reached out to the rest of the world from their forested isolation. They built schools, taught their children and each other, erected churches, and prayed variously to their God. Charles Robert Pratsch, part-time photographer, a man among them, has preserved a collection of images of that time, and some of them are presented in the following pages.

In the last half of the nineteenth century, the great forests of the Pacific Northwest were one of the last remaining areas in the United States still rich in investment potential. To its borders came the innocent, the steadfast, the righteous, the bold, the cunning, the ruthless, and the spoilers. Each came to redeem what he believed to be the great American promise.

Dreams of wealth for certain heavy investors on Grays Harbor were well realized, but to many eager pioneer settlers — the homesteaders, the small businessmen, loggers and mill hands, the sailors and the fishermen — it was often a legacy of failed dreams, spent lives, anger, and frustration.

The people fastened their anticipation of good fortune on the seaward extension of the railways to Grays Harbor. That, they believed, would transform the harbor into a major Northwest seaport. They were not alone in such aspirations; almost every Northwest coastal community hoped for the railway to terminate in its town, and too many people bought and sold land and planned factories and towns as though it had already happened. The Northern Pacific Railway was extending north from the Columbia River to Puget Sound, and after considering a number of alternative locations, decided to build their first seaward terminus at Tacoma, to the despair of Seattle. There were civic wounds and disappointments in Port Townsend, Port Angeles, Astoria, Grays Harbor, and other towns, too.

The problem in the Grays Harbor country was to reach the markets for their wood products and fish. The railway would have helped solve many problems, but it never came at the right time or in the places it was most needed. When it did arrive, the railroad did not have the strong financial support to make the harbor into a major shipping point. The sea was the answer, and it had to be exploited efficiently. The infant villages on the harbor became dependent on the sea, and the early history of these little mill towns is marked strongly by the sea, sea trades, shipbuilding, seamen, and seafaring.

Grays Harbor country was the lumberman's virtual heaven. A particularly famous tract of Douglas fir, a six-mile-square area locally known as 21-9, was so densely wooded that is was logged continually for more than thirty years. This profitable natural resource had lain substantially ignored until the latter half of the nineteenth century when the concentrated energies and the full storm of capital investment burst upon it.

What the citizens of the tiny mill towns on Grays Harbor knew too little about was the extent to which the lands on which they lived and worked were controlled by certain large financial syndicates and corporations. In the lumber sector it was most of all Pope & Talbot Lumber Company and its far-flung subsidiary empire, while in the railroad sector it was the Northern Pacific Railway. For the economic life of an area that was a single industrial unit, totally dependent on lumbering for its life, the corporate power of lumber and rail interests to dominate and control proved dangerous. From its forming days until well into the early 1900s Grays Harbor country should be described as a huge, profitably run company town. The interminable struggle against such an economic stranglehold produced small and temporary victories for some, and a handful of men became wealthy serving corporate interests, even unwittingly in some cases. For thousands of workmen and small businessmen for whom life in the area was a never-ending battle, the struggle seemed almost always to end in difficulty, if not in defeat.

These prolonged series of confrontations between corporate strength and workers resulted in unceasing economic warfare, moving in turn to labor organization, exploding into violence and reaction at intervals, crystallizing at times into political reaction, as witness Ku Klux Klan control of Aberdeen's city government in 1925. Bursting into uncommon fury along this path were the publicized brutalities of Centralia and Everett, Washington, and the lynch justice practiced against Wobblies by the well-remembered company union, the 4 L's, the Loyal Legion of Lumbermen and Loggers.

Unspared by nature's savagery, beaten time and again by economic forces they did not understand, angered into bitterness by enemies dimly perceived, thwarted in their dreams for a better life by economic domination they could not possibly overcome, the common people of Grays Harbor battled nature and each other. It is small wonder that this tree-rich wonderland in southwestern Washington should breed the social tensions and social violence that inspired novelists, journalists, reformers, and historians to regard the area with apprehension and awe.

THE FIVE RIVERS

Five rivers flow into and form Grays Harbor. The largest of them, the Chehalis,* rises on the westernmost flank of the Cascade Mountains and flows west into Grays Harbor on its passage to the Pacific. Joining the Chehalis at Grays Harbor are three small rivers, the Wishkah, Hoquiam, and Humptulips. They all drain twisted courses southward from their origins in the Olympic foothills north from the bay. Farther to the east a fifth river, the Wynoochee, southward flowing, adds its flow of fresh water. Cutting their ways south and west, scouring their bottoms as they run, the five rivers heavy with silt and debris deposit their sediment all along their courses, leaving permanent and shifting sandbars in their wakes. Aided by eight-and-one-half-foot tides, the hidden and visible bars present dangerous obstructions to both seagoing and river traffic.

At the sea mouth of the Chehalis is the Grays Harbor bar, as murderous, most of the time, as other infamous Pacific Coast bars. Safe passage here required both a skillful bar pilot and a sturdy tugboat. The wrong combination of strong seas and heavy winds could prove fatal to ships and sailors. It was no picnic, crossing that bar, and it was justly feared.

The Chehalis was navigable from the sea, twenty-five miles upriver to Montesano, a town at the head of tidewater. On the banks of the Chehalis' course westward and downriver were in turn the towns of Cosmopolis on the south shore, and on the north shore Junction City, Aberdeen, Hoquiam, and Grays Harbor City. Westport on the south shore, near the ocean, was the harbor's major terminus for riverboat traffic.

The slowly widening, westward-flowing Chehalis was split in the bay into three navigable channels, North, South, and the most easily navigated Middle Channel. Shifting sandbars, as well as two larger, mid-river islands, Sand Island and Rennie Island, acted as channel dividers. The south shore sired Stearns Bluff, the infant City of Grays Harbor, Ocosta-by-the-Sea, and various fledging communities. Well to the east, South Aberdeen, a slowly developing adjunct to its parent, justified the succession of "swing" bridges built across the river to join the two areas.

HOQUIAM

One of the two oldest communities on Grays Harbor, Hoquiam was built on the west bank of the Hoquiam River where it joins the Chehalis. Located on deep river water, the town is twelve miles from the Pacific Ocean. This pioneer settlement was founded in

---

* Pronounced Chehalis, not Kehalis.

1859 by James Karr and his family, who were quickly joined by four brothers, Scotsmen named Campbell. The infant settlement grew slowly, opening a post office in 1869 and a school in 1873. The Hoquiam River was a blessing even though its rank tideflats were a menace to shipping. Thirty feet deep upriver for three miles from its mouth, it was navigable by smaller steamers for an additional fifteen miles, a great advantage to loggers and sawmills farther from the bay. The Northwestern Lumber Company, established by George H. Emerson for Captain Asa M. Simpson, was the pioneer sawmill on the Hoquiam, cutting its first lumber in September 1882. It attracted business interests and settlers, enabling the town to be platted successfully in 1885 with a permanent population of two hundred to three hundred residents. Interestingly, all early land sales in Hoquiam obliged the purchaser to build upon it, while mill people and certain public-spirited citizens donated parcels of land for manufacturing enterprises. Civic vigor was much in evidence in early Hoquiam.

1889 proved a peak year there. Attracted by increased railroad intimations that Grays Harbor *might* be the ocean terminus, a flow of immigrants, beginning in June, increased the town's population of four hundred to fifteen hundred by year's end.

Hoquiam was a third-class incorporated city with two sawmills, three churches and one school, four hotels, a $150,000 electric lighting plant, two miles of planked streets (planked over slabwood fill and sawdust), five miles of planked sidewalks, mail delivery once a day, and transport three times a day west to Grays Harbor City. A river trip on the steamer *Montesano*, three miles upriver to Aberdeen, cost twenty-five cents. The Northwestern Lumber Company was cutting 100,000 board feet of lumber daily, and schooners waited their turn in the bay to load their cargoes. The cacophony of whining saws, screaming wood, and shrieking whistles rarely ceased. The little town was a scene of constant activity night and day. Lumbering dominated the town as it grew. Hoquiam literally huddled around the three pioneer mills — the Northwestern, the E. K. Wood, and the Hoquiam Lumber and Shingle Company — all on the upper west shore, the flat bank of the Hoquiam River. The mills were the prime customers of the town electric plant. Wooden shipbuilding grew rapidly, with the mill providing on the spot the finest timber available. They attracted some of the best shipbuilders on the Pacific Coast: John Joyce, G. H. Hitchings, and Peter and G. F. Matthews, father and son. The launchings of vessels from these yards into the Hoquiam River were town galas, attracting the entire population as often as not. The town grew and developed west and north from the river, since the lack of deep water on the bayfront prevented vessels from lying alongside in safety.

Along with Aberdeen, Hoquiam failed in its initial efforts to sell its land to the Northern Pacific Railway for building through the two towns. It was only in 1899, four years after Aberdeen's initial success in linking up with the railroad, that Hoquiam secured rail linkage for its mills. That four-year head start for Aberdeen proved decisive; Hoquiam never overcame that economic lead.

GRAYS HARBOR CITY

Early in 1889, Eastern capitalists organized the Grays Harbor Company and in March bought four bayfront miles of land under Breckenridge's Bluff three miles west of Hoquiam on the north shore. They platted, graded, and cleared space for a new bay port to be called Grays Harbor City. They built a mile-long trestle out over the tideflats into the deep water of the north channel in April, and by July 20, 1889, lots were offered for sale to the public. Greed was at a fever pitch, and no lot went for less than $500. Investors in nearby Hoquiam became so excited that they built a $100,000 white elephant, the Hoquiam Hotel, to attract an anticipated flood of visitors. A certain railroad financier, George W. Hunt of Walla Walla, projected a rail line from Centralia, to Grays Harbor City, passing through Hoquiam on its way west. It was planned to carry coal from Centralia and wheat from eastern Washington to Grays Harbor City, from whence they would be shipped by sea, along with Grays Harbor lumber, to San Francisco and other destinations. Together, this volume, Hunt hoped, would transform Grays Harbor into the leading shipping port in the Pacific Northwest. Proposing to complete the railroad by August of 1891, Hunt collected a $500,000 subsidy from the towns of Grays Harbor City and Hoquiam. The railroad was never built, the real estate bubble burst, and the anticipated fortunes of the infant communities never materialized. Mr. George Hunt, financier and railroad builder, was long remembered in Grays Harbor.

COSMOPOLIS

A few miles east of Aberdeen the brawling town of Cosmopolis, nicknamed by loggers the "Western Penitentiary," lives on in remembered notoriety. It was, at its height, an infamous example of a lumber-company town, and its reputation was scandalous for recruiting cheap labor not only in the Pacific Northwest but all across middle America.

Cosmopolis is one of the oldest settlements on the harbor. Its first white settlers were James Pilkington and his brother in the early 1850s. Located on the Chehalis River, three and one-half miles upstream from Aberdeen on the south shore, the town had to build out of the dense forest surrounding it. Pilkington embittered the local Indians and left the area, selling everything he owned to David Bayles and Austin Young. They platted the town, Samuel James Jr. named it Cosmopolis, and it was recorded on June 25, 1861.

Tanning from hemlock bark was tried first, but the difficulties in reaching a market forced an end to the effort. Mill Creek was then dammed and a flume-powered grist mill was built. Unable to keep wheat dry in the perpetually dank atmosphere, the mill never succeeded, and John Fry, a millwright and the grist mill's original builder, converted the lower floor into a water-powered sawmill in 1879. It cut only cedar and produced no more than four to five thousand board feet a day; yet the mill's first lumber was shipped in 1881 to Portland aboard the two-masted schooner *Kate and Ann*. By 1882 John Fry once again converted the little sawmill to a steam-powered mill by the addition of a boiler, increasing its capacity to thirty thousand board feet per day.

Forty acres were slashed in 1883, and the town started to grow as shacks, stores, and hotels were built on the townsite. Business was booming in 1885 all over the harbor as everything seemed to mushroom. People came, land was cleared, the mills were enlarged, shipping increased, and Cosmopolis emerged as an important lumber-cutting mill town on the harbor.

For mill owners the central problem in the 1880s was securing a steady, dependable supply of logs, cheaply and competitively. Farmers clearing their land were happy to sell logs to the mills for what it cost them to put the logs in the water. In 1887 in Grays Harbor, the prevailing price was $4.50 to $5.50 per thousand feet for logs, whereas on Puget Sound it ranged from $5.50 to $7.00 per thousand feet. Grays Harbor mills could offer rough-sawn lumber at the price Puget Sound mills had to pay for logs.

This significant advantage convinced Puget Sound's lumber kings, Pope & Talbot Lumber Company, to look for a mill on Grays Harbor. But the firm refusal of Grays Harbor mill owners to join a Pope & Talbot–controlled pricing and merchandising consortium, operating in San Francisco as the Pacific Pine & Lumber Company, thwarted this plan. The Pacific Pine & Lumber Company, a consortium of eleven mill companies, was persuaded by W. H. Talbot to operate its own competing mill on Grays Harbor. They proposed to W. H. Perry of the Perry Lumber & Mill Company in Los Angeles that he sell them the original Anderson mill at Cosmopolis. He rejected the proposed purchase summarily. The consortium, angered by the refusal, rebuffed in their attempt to gain a foothold at Grays Harbor, countered swiftly. They bought a quarter section of land near Cosmopolis and ordered mill machinery, assigning George Stetson, one of the Company members, to begin construction immediately.

The threat proved effective. Perry capitulated quickly, selling the mill to the consortium in July 1888. Although Stetson had already built a warehouse and staked out a millsite, plans to continue construction were dropped. The sale solidly established the consortium at Grays Harbor as well as giving Pope & Talbot, soon to become a controlling stockholder, a firm location on Grays Harbor for the first time.

Although the new mill was originally named the Grays Harbor Mill Company, it was renamed the Grays Harbor Commercial Company in 1895. It retained that name until its demise late in 1929. The eleven original stockholders in the consortium, the Pacific Pine & Lumber Company, eventually relinquished their participation in the venture, their stock passing to Pope & Talbot Company. Full control of the Cosmopolis mill by them was thus assured.

1888 was a good time for lumbering in the Northwest. Economic developments were booming and the settlements at both Aberdeen and Hoquiam were firmly on their way. Demands for building materials swelled, the depleted Eastern forests proved unable to meet the needs, shipping as well as shipping facilities increased. California became a profitable high-demand market, and money for expansion of the mill at Cosmopolis became available.

The first train of the newly arrived Northern Pacific Railway turned on the wye and backed into Cosmopolis in May of 1892. Its economic impact was immediate, creating new opportunities for the mill. From Cosmopolis it was only forty miles east to the rail line at Centralia, then sixty miles north to the deep-water port of Tacoma, and the railroad hastened to point out the advantages to lumber shippers. Expansion became the order of the day at Cosmopolis. But unlike Aberdeen, Hoquiam, and Montesano — who offered investors liberal inducements of land and credit, encouraging competition — Pope & Talbot did *not* offer any sort of advantages to manufacturers. They were not interested in sharing their business interests in Cosmopolis where they owned everything — stores, messhouses, bunkhouses. Competition was neither encouraged nor allowed.

The sawmill at Cosmopolis went on two shifts a day; to the mill were added a box and tank factory, planing mills, drying kilns, and two shingle mills. The entire complex employed twelve hundred men at its height. From cutting 30,000 board feet per day in 1881, the mill increased its capacity in seven years to 600,000 board feet per day.

Wages were low, and they were kept that way. For a ten-hour day a skilled man could expect company-furnished board and thirty-five to forty dollars a month. Labor was recruited steadily in Seattle, and the turnover was great. Favors were neither expected nor given. Men came to Cosmopolis to work hard and long, make their stake, and get out. There were not many loggers in the Northwest who had not "put their time in" at Cosmopolis. It was a low-wage heaven for skid-row down-and-outers and was known as such in every hobo jungle of the day. Race, creed, or color did not matter at Cosmopolis; anyone who would work for low wages and keep his mouth shut on the job was welcome. Cheap labor was needed, and Cosmopolis was organized to use it profitably, and that was all. Most of the work was unskilled, and all of it was dangerous. The food was the plainest, and low-paid Chinese cooks prepared it. Conditions were the poorest, and no money was spent by the company to improve them.

It was not simply that the mills at Cosmopolis were so much larger than any other or better equipped, or that the consortium owned so many more ships to deliver the lumber sawn there, or even that the marketing and distribution arrangements they could organize among themselves were so much more profitable. The reputation of Cosmopolis as a rough, tough company town—rougher than any other—rested on different foundations. Every second that men worked and every ounce of labor expended there had to pay handsomely; it was drive, drive, drive, every minute of every working hour. The pressure in the sawmills anywhere was severe; in the mills at Cosmopolis it was almost unendurable. It was designed to squeeze out of every man the utmost that he could give, then cast him out, often badly wounded in both body and spirit. Few mill workers could stand it at Cosmopolis for very long. In all respects, Cosmopolis deserved its reputation as Pope & Talbot's company town.

By 1900 the Grays Harbor Commercial Company at Cosmopolis was producing more lumber than any other sawmill on Grays Harbor. Nine million feet were cut in 1900, an astonishing figure for any sawmill on the Coast. Three million of it were shipped by rail and six million by water, all to be sold at the Pope & Talbot Third Street yard in San Francisco. By 1929 this mill, this yard, this company at Cosmopolis were closed down.

ABERDEEN

Grays Harbor's jewel, its manufacturing and shipping center, was, and is, Aberdeen, sixteen miles from the sea at the head of the harbor where the Wishkah, cutting the town into two parts, joins the Chehalis. Located on the tidewater, built on a narrow shelf of land, the town rises from the water in a gentle slope, leveling off to an indefinite plateau of about fifty or seventy-five feet. It was almost hidden by low hills thick with tall trees before the trees were cut down.

Aberdeen was lucky in its founder, Samuel Benn. A young Irishman, he brought to his enterprises a liberal outlook, a generosity of spirit, and a keen recognition that in the conduct of business, a respect for the other fellow's self-interest promotes greater cooperation all around than tight-fisted selfishness. He arrived in Grays Harbor with his cousin, George Hubbard, from San Francisco in 1859, settling on a farm at short-lived Melbourne in June of that year. In 1865 he traded his Chehalis River bottom land to his father-in-law, Reuben Redman, for 600 acres in present-day Aberdeen. He bought 140 acres more from a disgruntled settler and brought his family to the area in 1868. This nameless dense forest, this 740 uncleared acres at the junction of the Chehalis and the Wishkah, became the cradle of Sam Benn's unflagging dream of a commercial center on the harbor.

From the beginning, Sam Benn spared no energy or any wise generosity to expand the area and attract settlers and investors. The first decade was a grueling and lonely one, but by 1873 an Astorian, George W. Hume came to Aberdeen looking for a site to build a fish cannery. He accepted Benn's gift of land in Aberdeen and opened the first large cannery on the harbor. The town was platted on February 16, 1884, recorded in 1884, and in 1888 the owners of the Aberdeen Packing Company received permission to name the new town. They named it Aberdeen after the home in Scotland of some of their stockholders as the proposed name Wishkah was considered unsuitable. James Stout was named postmaster when the town secured a post office in 1884. He and his successor, John Fairfield, served only briefly and were succeeded in 1885 by Charles Augustus Pratsch, father of our artist-photographer, Charles Robert Pratsch. He served until 1889. The year 1884 witnessed the opening of the first store and the arrival of the first physician. Aberdeen in 1882 had been completely covered with timber, and by March 1890 it had become a small city with a population of two thousand, even though in 1884 it had been no more than a raw clearing in the forest with only six lonesome buildings on it—a cannery, the Aberdeen house, a store, a saloon, and two residences. To understand Aberdeen's potential for wealth, consider that in 1900 there were fifty billion feet of merchantable lumber standing on eighty thousand acres of river-bottom land around Aberdeen. All of it stood close to good driving water; rivers running fast enough to carry logs.

Sam Benn knew this from the beginning, and so did A. J West, a Michigan lumberman, who came to Aberdeen in June 1884 because he had heard that Benn was offering sawmill sites and special advantages for any takers. West set up a sawmill, and even though by July the mill had neither roof nor walls, the machinery was in place, and it was cutting timber. It was Aberdeen's first, attracting Captain John M. Weatherwax, who purchased land on the west bank and established his own sawmill on the spot. The town organized for expansion in 1885, electing a Town Council and setting up a Board of Trade in 1889 that promptly advertised their great pride in the growing metropolis.

Railroad development figured large in Aberdeen's growth. The Tacoma, Olympia, and Grays Harbor Railroad was built southward from Tacoma in 1890 to Montesano on the north shore of the Chehalis River. The new line linked up with the Northern Pacific Railway, which was building new tracks to a Pacific Coast terminus still unannounced publicly. Coming just one year after the ill-fated railway line proposed by George Hunt to Hoquiam and Grays Harbor City, the Aberdeen city fathers schemed to entice the line from Montesano to Aberdeen. Fate was against them, for the new railroad pushed west from Montesano along the north shore to Junction City, a stone's throw east of Aberdeen. There, instead of proceeding to Aberdeen, it turned south crossing the Chehalis over the newly completed steel bridge at Junction City into Cosmopolis on the south shore. There an exultant population of four hundred and fifty and a twenty-piece band loudly cheered Engine No. 99, John Dasher, engineer, as the first train backed into Cosmopolis in May 1892.

This opened up the curious, short-lived saga of Ocosta-by-the-Sea, so named by joining the Spanish La Costa (the coast) with an enthusiastic "O." Having crossed the Chehalis on the south side of the river at Cosmopolis, bypassing the north shore towns, Colonel F. D. Heustis, the railroad's building contractor in charge, announced that the newly founded village of Ocosta, on the south side of the harbor, would be the Northern Pacific's new terminus at Grays Harbor. Ocosta's prospects boomed astronomically almost overnight. On May 1, 1890, some three hundred of the new town's platted lots sold for a total of $100,000.

Hard times in 1893, lack of expected federal support for needed dredging of the south channel, and the crippling railroad strike of 1894 forced the withdrawal of many Ocosta residents to seek better prospects elsewhere. All these combined to diminish Ocosta's worth to the Northern Pacific as their rail terminus on Grays Harbor. Although Aberdeen citizens subsequently rejected a Northern Pacific request that *they* subsidize the building of a rail line to Aberdeen for $35,000, the more public-spirited among them proposed instead building a railroad line *themselves* at less cost. This could then be turned over to the Northern Pacific, cutting out as well the town's major competitor, Hoquiam, from sharing in its advantage. This venture was a small model of farsightedness by Aberdeen's business community and citizens.

Five thousand pieces of railroad track salvaged from the British bark *Abercorn,* which had run aground at the north entrance to Grays Harbor in June 1888, were purchased at a delinquent tax sale by three Aberdeen businessmen, headed by mill owner Weatherwax, and donated to the railroad project. The Aberdeen lumbermen, Weatherwax, A. J. West, and Henry Wilson, donated ties, and the town's generous founder, Samuel Benn, offered free lots to any volunteer who donated either ten days' labor or ten days' pay at two dollars per day. In addition, he donated land on what is now East Wishkah Street to be used for the mill yard and the train depot. The responses in Aberdeen from all quarters were generous, the line was completed, and on June 1, 1895, the finished track was formally turned over to the Northern Pacific. The first train arrived in Aberdeen shortly thereafter. The extension of the new railroad to Hoquiam in 1899, replacing the planked road built in 1888–90 between the two towns, and its evident successes for the north shore towns guaranteed the eventual demise of the south shore town Ocosta-by-the-Sea. By 1910 it was reduced to nearly a ghost town, a monument to greed, manipulation, and mismanagement.

Aberdeen grew as the lumber business on the harbor expanded. Mills increased in number and in capacity, crowding the entire Chehalis waterfront from Hoquiam to Cosmopolis. Some of the more notable were the West Mill, the Slade Mill, the Wilson Lumber Co., the Aberdeen Lumber and Shingle Co., the Weatherwax Mill, the F. E. Jones Shingle Co., and the Bay City Lumber Co. in South Aberdeen. In 1900, with a population of only 3747, Aberdeen boasted six sawmills, two shingle mills, one stave factory, one cooperage, and two shipyards; the one belonging to Aberdeen's shipbuilding mayor, Johnny Lindstrom, was the more important. The mills' daily output was 450,000 board feet of lumber, and in 1900 the staggering total of 250 million logs was delivered to the mills.

The monthly payroll in Aberdeen averaged $100,000, and ample palaces of pleasure were provided for its workers to spend it in. Few seaports of the world were without their "hell streets," and in Aberdeen it was Heron and F Streets bordering the west bank of the Wishkah. Sailors and loggers knew this area as their own private pleasure ground, and it was deservedly notorious. They boldly staked out this dangerous tideflat as theirs alone, spending their money with abandon, drinking wildly, carousing and gambling in grand style. The dangerous play the loggers knew as relaxation raged on day and night, sailors and loggers fighting in the streets. Laughingly called "The Sailor's Paradise," this sordid hellhole in Aberdeen needed only saloons and brothels and it had them in dizzying abundance. The "Line," as the narrow dirt street was called, housed a long row of tawdry saloons, brothels, sailors' outfitting stores, cheap tailor shops, squalid boarding houses, shipping offices, and the local headquarters of the Sailors Union of the Pacific. More than half these buildings had second floors with suitable rooms and ladies of the night to match.

Lining the street in 1908 were such infamous dens as Heffron's Saloon, the Lion, Log Cabin, Brook Saloon, Fashion Saloon, Our House, Pioneer Bar, Mint Saloon, Grant Saloon, Twin Saloon, Merry Widow (with rooms upstairs), Diamond Front, Palm Dance Hall, Corner Whale, My House, Bonita, and the Klondike Saloon. Two of the most notorious were the Humboldt Saloon and the Grant, the latter housing the Sailors Union office upstairs and its infamous agent Billy Gohl. He was sent to prison for the one murder of which he was found guilty, although he boasted of twenty-odd for which he was never brought to justice.

This part of Aberdeen was wild, flamboyant, wide open, and murderously dangerous. Seafaring men who visited the "Line" in Aberdeen and tasted its dubious delights never forgot it, nor did the loggers who dreamed of its sinful joy. Loggers called their pay "pleasure money," and an observer has been quoted about the loggers' conduct here: "From their language one would think their mothers were not women."

If Aberdeen had its wild side, it was still a town, the biggest on Grays Harbor. It had three schools, six hundred and fifty pupils, fifteen teachers, and two hospitals—one private and one run by the Sisters of Charity. Fish canning, encouraged by Samuel Benn, had grown into a serious business involving three major facilities. The Chehalis and nearby rivers contributed salmon: silver and hookjaw were the tastiest and the most valuable. From the ocean nearby came cod and halibut. The town sported two theaters, one for vaudeville and the other limited to "first-class attractions" only. The first fire department, a bucket brigade, was started in 1888. This civic function struggled to meet the major threat ever-present in any lumbering community: fire. To a mill town in the 1900s built of wood and surrounded by wood, as was Aberdeen, the losses from fire could be catastrophic, a major economic disaster. Imagine a town with streets and sidewalks filled with sawdust and planked over with wood! The entire business section of Aberdeen was destroyed in October 1903 by a major fire after an equally serious fire the previous year. The wooden buildings were replaced fourteen months later by structures of brick, stone, cement, and mortar. By 1907 the wooden sidewalks were finally replaced by cement, and city fire regulations firmly prevented the building of new wooden business structures in Aberdeen.

There was more to life on Grays Harbor than man-killing labor, bitter weather, social violence, and economic disaster. Many early families kept gardens, chickens, and cattle, providing nutritious food and work at home for all. Picnics and parties were organized often, outings by river steamer to Westport topped all other pleasures. Berrying in the woods was popular, as was clamming on the ocean beaches. There was social visiting between families, and homemade entertainment was amply provided. Music, self-made music, loomed large in the social life of the area, supporting choral groups of merit, small orchestras, and bands of lusty vigor.

Overriding all these pleasures were the neighborliness and the satisfactions in mutually sharing an interdependence forced upon them by the isolation, the meager sources of supplies, and the harsh environment of early southwestern Washington Territory. The comforting presence of almost every type of church in the mill towns afforded great satisfaction as well as the joy of regular human contact. Every possible opportunity for town festivities, from ship launchings to new construction, was seized upon, and certain national holidays were near riotous in the frenzies they unleashed.

Despite their interdependence, the rich and the poor lived separately, in desirable and less desirable portions of the towns, and the segregation of the "native, white Americans" from the foreigners — the Finns, Serbs, Croats, and others — split the little communities as they grew into further social strata. The tensions created by these discriminating structures often underlay the passions unleashed in intermittent attempts at labor organization and the resistance they engendered.

Labor violence, endemic to the lumber business, followed in the wake of organized efforts by the workers to improve their wages and their conditions. In general, these efforts followed the economic fortunes of the harbor. When the lumber markets were booming, as in 1912, trade union activity was high. During World War I the Industrial Workers of the World, the "Wobblies," in concert with shipyard workers, were very effective in winning many supporters on Grays Harbor. During hard times, as in the depression of 1907, the unions and their temporary gains were decimated, and in 1917 the formation on Grays Harbor of an effective company union, the 4 L's — which has been described as a vigilante group as well — dealt crippling blows to the trade unions, particularly the I.W.W. The savagery of those struggles became the subject of several vigorous novels, and certain logger victims of those harsh times are now remembered as labor martyrs, heroes of the class war.

The developing twentieth century brought sharp changes to the area and its wood-products industries. Muscle and brute strength no longer dominated the scene; machines proved more dependable and more powerful. Even more importantly for investors, productivity per man increased notably, and profits soared. Steam-powered vessels replaced sailing lumber carriers at sea for the same reasons, and in place of the time-honored logging railroads in the woods, paved roads and massive lumber trucks became commonplace. Replacing Neil Cooney's screaming mill at Cosmopolis, there now stands an automated mill, no longer Pope & Talbot's pride and joy, but Weyerhaeuser's.

New times force new ideas upon us all, as well as new solutions. The view backward grows misty and vague. The skill and insight of our photographers, Charles Robert Pratsch and his colleauges, allow us a clear view of the way it looked when promise was high for eager men and women in the Grays Harbor country.

The Harbor and the Rivers

Flanked by Puget Sound to the north and the great Columbia River forty miles to the south, Grays Harbor remains one of the few natural harbors on Washington's ocean frontier. Ringed on both shores by dense stands of tall trees, the harbor had been an isolated spot sheltering only animals and savage mosquitoes in droves before Europeans came to settle and exploit its abundant timber resources. Earlier, Pacific Coast Indians had come singly and in groups to its ocean beaches to fish and clam. Their great war canoes, carved and burnt out of Douglas firs, are eloquent witness to their dependence on Washington timber.

The first white men to enter the harbor as settlers came over the mountains following river valleys to the Chehalis, the broad river that forms the harbor. The trek was hard, for there were few trails, the hills were steep, and every foot of the way was choked with dense underbrush. The original settlers realized that only the most determined would follow them to the harbor. It didn't take them long to realize that unless

In Grays Harbor the forests dominated every horizon except westward to the sea. The vastness stretching in all directions dwarfed everything by comparison. Hurrying to pick up a waiting vessel, a little tugboat rushes past the Aberdeen Shingle and Lumber Company mills and two big four-mast schooners waiting at the mill dock to load their cargoes.

they did something to improve the way people and goods came to Grays Harbor, they were doomed to isolation. The problem was to find or create an easier way into the harbor.

Most of their day-to-day problems were really one large problem demanding a practical solution: How were they to establish regular contact with the rest of Washington Territory and, beyond it, the world outside? They needed neighbors, markets, and additional resources — human contact most of all, for their loneliness was hard to bear.

They had two main choices. One way was to build roads to the harbor and thus make overland travel easier. The towns they needed to be in touch with were not far geographically. There were Seattle and Tacoma to the north and Portland to the southwest in Oregon Territory. But having to depend exclusively on primitive overland transport and poor roads to get back and forth could not be the answer. Little more than dim trails led through the forests. The early roads were poorly built, and upkeep was largely nonexistent. Inns for people and forage stops for tired animals were few and far between. To take the overland option would require endless work and great expense, only prolonging their isolation and leaving Grays Harbor still remote and little-visited. The other way was to utilize the rivers and the sea as their highways.

The settlers in Aberdeen and Hoquiam decided to favor the rivers and the sea. The choice was not made in any sort of council; no vote was recorded for or against. It was more a matter of taking the easy way, perhaps no more than continuing a path they were already using. The Pacific Ocean entrance lay between Point Damon on the north spit and Peterson's Point on the south and thence up the Chehalis to Hoquiam and Aberdeen on the river's north shore. Until the railroads came, it was the easiest and best way.

Grays Harbor, sixteen miles long from its head to its ocean mouth and twelve miles across at its widest point, is in fact no more than a flowing river that broadens as it forces its way downstream to the Pacific. Together with the four smaller rivers emptying into it on their southward courses, the harbor offered many advantages to settlers. It was natural enough that towns were founded where the smaller rivers joined the slow-moving Chehalis, each village stretching north and west along its glistening tideflats. Thus the village of Hoquiam was located only three impassable miles west of Aberdeen along the banks of the Hoquiam River, Aberdeen was along the Chehalis flats at its juncture with the Wishkah, and Montesano bordered the twisted Chehalis twenty miles to the east.

Although the towns originally included many settlers who came to farm, the mark of the sea upon each of them was obvious. The dominant trades apart from logging, sawmilling, and farming were all related to the sea. Shipbuilding, ship suppliers, saloons, boarding houses, brothels, and fish canneries outnumbered all others from the first. Many local citizens were ships' officers, sailors, shipbuilders, fishermen, tugboaters, and riverboatmen. The towns belonged as much to its transient seafarers as it did to its farmers and loggers. Indeed, for some the jobs were interchangeable according to the season.

Everyone on the harbor depended on the sea for a living in one way or another. A large part of what the town produced left in the holds or on the decks of ships, just as what was needed for work and living came back in the same way, and often in the same ships.

The harbor and the rivers meant a great deal to the early settlers since they depended on them for transport, recreation, and food. The harbor and rivers offered fortunes for a few who invested in the future, a decent, hard-working livelihood for many, and only a wet, dreary existence for an embittered few. The rivers were used by everyone differently. For some they were a highway of dreams to be used to advantage, while for others they were forever a wet nightmare. The photographs reveal the variety of activities that dotted both shores of every river mile into the harbor towns, although they cannot as clearly reveal the river's many dangers. All sixteen muddy miles of the Chehalis from its sea mouth to where it narrowed at the head of the harbor were treacherous. It was shallow, and the sandbars to be seen at low tide menaced shipping. Hidden at high tide and shifting at every flooding runoff, they were a nuisance to sailors searching for the familiar marked channels. Rank tidal flats easily located by their odor bordered both shores of the harbor. As a consequence of an eight-and-one-half-foot tide, many of the town's structures built out over the flats rocked uneasily each time the tide rose and fell.

Navigation through the harbor required intimate knowledge of the river's bottom or the skills of a local pilot. In a pinch a sober fisherman served as well and was often used. In spite of local help, strandings on the Chehalis' sandbars were common, providing work for the local tugboatmen, and their tiny steam tugs. It took a while for shipmasters to accept the need for tugs, but as more ships and crews were lost on the ocean beaches, swept ashore by the breaking sea bar there, the severe truth of their need for help was finally grasped.

In spite of many such problems, the harbor grew more popular. In the variety of what went on there, it presented many different faces to viewers, an endlessly changing picture, rarely lacking in a kind of rugged attraction. The way in from the ocean led past sawmills filling the sky with smoke, while booms of freshly felled trees waited in the river to be cut up into useful lumber. Sailing vessels bobbed alongside mill docks loading the one cargo they carried endlessly, Grays Harbor prime lumber. Tugboats, gillnetters, river steamers, and small sailboats scooted about the river like dragonflies on a millpond, filling the air with the varied sounds of their passages, upstream or down.

The harbor, for all of its isolation from the mainstream of coast shipping, was a noisy place, the sound of steam whistles filling the air, gulls hawking shrilly, men shouting and cursing as they worked, and everywhere the sweet smell of fresh-sawn wood. This harbor was a busy highway for water-borne commerce designed to fascinate onlookers as only ships and sailors could.

Take the journey upriver yourself; the photographs can help you enjoy it.

For a long time a popular way in and out of the Harbor was its sea-path, an ocean entrance not always as calm as it seems here. Aberdeen's favorite steam tug, John Cudahy, eases the four-mast schooner En-deavour, bound in to load lum-ber, over the now quiet, still dangerous, sea bar.

Below: *A few shipwrecks often dotted the beaches north and south of the ocean entrance. The British four-mast bark Poltalloch, built in Belfast in 1893 by Workman and Clark and Co., piled ashore one bad night, all standing, even the sails on her* *foreyards still hastily clewed up. The effort seen here to tow her off the beach and back into deep water was successful. She carried cargoes on the Pacific Coast for American owners for years afterwards.*

Opposite: *High and dry at Copalis Beach, twelve miles north of Grays Harbor, the three-mast schooner Charles E. Falk lies stranded, March 31, 1909. Her crew of eight was saved, and the vessel was eventually hauled off the beach and returned to service for her owner, N. H. Falk of Eureka, California.*

The way upriver, east to the harbor's towns, passed a succession of sawmills, loading docks, schooners, barkentines, and little steam schooners, each ship's captain impatient to be loaded and off to California ports.

Opposite top: *A classic Grays Harbor view: smoking sawmills, loading ships, silvered rivers, and discarded stumps of felled trees as grotesque reminders of the forest. The photograph can only suggest the accompanying sounds that added life—screaming saws, hoarse steam whistles, squealing blocks, and hawking gulls.*

Opposite bottom: *Those approaching Aberdeen from the west saw skies filled night and day with steam and smoke from working mills and passing steamboats. In the evenings it could appear like an inferno.*

Because lumber meant money for so many, it dominated every harbor view. It all began with felled trees assembled outside the sawmills, bobbing endlessly in the crowded log booms, waiting to be dragged up the mill ramp to the cutting saws.

Sometimes the trees in the log boom were so thick they blotted out the pond. Packed so tightly, they look as though they could be safely walked on, a trick tried by many youngsters in spite of repeated warnings.

Only A. J. West's pioneer saw-mill on the Wishkah's east bank and the passing steam tug Ranger, bound upriver, break the isolation and the wet silence in this view of early-day Aberdeen in 1885.

Opposite top: Overloaded with sightseers anxious to visit Teddy Roosevelt's Great White Fleet in 1907, the tiny riverboat Skookum, every flag flying, makes her way downriver to the ocean beaches at Westport.

Opposite bottom: A dependable old workhorse, the sternwheeler Harbor Belle, guaranteed transport and communication. Like an old shoe, she was well worn, comfortable, and reliable, puffing and groaning as she worked.

Left: *Hoquiam's watery world in 1906. The town awakens in the morning light as the wooden swing bridge opens the river in the foreground to traffic. Beyond the Chehalis' muddy tideflats the watery wastes of the harbor stretch south and west to the Pacific beaches.*

Above: *Her waiting markets far to the south in California, a two-masted "firewood" schooner makes her way in the Hoquiam River under tow by the local steam tug Traveler. Carrying a deckload higher than her main rails, she creates a classic picture of Grays Harbor.*

Preparing to tow a boom of logs to the mills for cutting was proper work for Grays Harbor steam tugs, such as the Daring, built in 1904 by John Lindstrom at Aberdeen, a handsome example of her type.

Opposite top: The ships at Aberdeen on July 4, 1907, take on a festive air. There is no work in the harbor, and each vessel is dressed for the holiday, flying every flag, every bit of bunting she can muster.

Opposite bottom: Steam and sail at Grays Harbor competed to carry lumber. Few old sailing-ship men realized how completely and quickly tiny steamers like the G. C. Lindauer lying here at the mill dock, right, would drive big four-mast schooners like the A. B. Johnson from the trade forever.

Further upriver where the Wishkah meets the Chehalis at Aberdeen, the mill docks on both sides host vessels waiting for passengers and cargo—the tiny stern-wheeler Skookum, the steam schooner Grace Dollar, a four-mast schooner, and the barkentine Wrestler. A small launch at right passes downriver in midstream.

Opposite top: A ferry was needed in Aberdeen to cross the unbridged Wishkah River at Heron and G streets. Tiny and drab, underpowered and misshapen, the tiny stern-wheeler transported her fares safely. Although her passages across the 250-foot-wide river were short, she and her genial Master, Orlando Mitchell, commanded admiration and affection from the many fishermen and mill hands who depended upon her.

Opposite bottom: Steamboats abounded on the harbor's tiny rivers. This little one, her fore-boom rigged and ready for loading deck cargo, emerges from the morning mists that passed for good weather on Grays Harbor.

Widely known to Pacific Northwest loggers as "Neil Cooney's Empire" was Pope & Talbot's notorious company mill town, Cosmopolis, nicknamed the "Western Penitentiary," on the Chehalis' south shore east of Aberdeen.

A faithful packhorse, the stern-wheel steamer Montesano, built at Aberdeen in 1899, backs away from her Montesano dock upriver from Aberdeen. Her daily arrivals and departures, heralded noisily by her steam whistle, were omens of successful commercial activity.

Watching clam diggers at work on the Harbor's tide-swept beaches was a pleasant diversion for many visitors. Digging in the mud for clams could be an exciting and rewarding sport. But for those who depended on their catches each day for their living, it was only back-breaking labor, and smelly to boot. ►

The Towns and the Life

These photographs by Charles Robert Pratsch pose some questions difficult to answer conclusively. If they were made to be sold, who bought them? If, as seems likely, young Charles had only a few customers in the little tidewater villages of his time, why did he keep on making them? It was no small bother then, and the expense was far from slight.

It was not as simple in those days to take a photograph as it is today. There was much more to it than slinging a 35-mm. automatic camera around one's neck. Inasmuch as Charles Pratsch used 8″ × 10″ dry gelatin plates, together with a heavy view camera requiring a tripod, just getting this equipment to where it was needed often took a horse and buggy. A willingness to work and strong determination to make pictures were a must for any photographer, amateur or professional. To take photographs then for a living, successfully and profitably, was one thing; in that case such labor each day was justified. To produce the body of pictures we have here as a labor of love was quite another. What could have impelled this young photographer, who was only in his thirties when he started making these photographs, to record the minutiae of life in early-day Aberdeen and Hoquiam? We are still uncertain.

The view from the eastern hills behind Aberdeen was dazzling. It needed only a sensitive response to landscape to see and appreciate the river's primitive beauty, the spreading green forests, and the cloud-filled skies of Grays Harbor.

The pictures reveal that he was an accomplished photographer. His negatives and prints are sharp, well exposed, properly developed and printed. Although the posing of people for portraits was still very formal in his day, Pratsch's pictures project an unexpected quality of animation. The picnic scenes, for example, are as close to what we call "candid" as the lenses and emulsion of the day allowed. They suggest that it was the physical activity he saw that he wanted to capture, even though he knew he was able to make only "instantaneous" pictures, the kind in which only a slight degree of movement could be frozen satisfactorily by the camera's lens. The snapshot still awaited discovery, so he was denied the opportunity of portraying his world more accurately to generations to come. It is a pity, for we are thus denied images of a people for whom life was intensely physical. What Charles R. Pratsch may have regretted he could not show us in the lives of his neighbors we can only regret more today.

Information about Pratsch is scant. His distinctions were purely local, available records meager, and family recollections inadequate. He was born on November 17, 1857, in Lancaster, Pennsylvania, the eldest son of parents married only ten months. His father, Charles August Pratsch, was born in Leipzig in 1833 and died in 1898; his mother, Catherine Anna Dostman, was born in Lancaster in 1839 and died in 1920.

At the age of twenty-five young Charles left Iowa with his brother-in-law, Lester L. Darling, and arrived at Grays Harbor in 1882. They quickly homesteaded two adjacent claims on the Wishkah River in the brand-new town of Aberdeen, platted in 1883, and formally organized in 1885. After establishing their claims legally in 1884, they were joined that same year by the elder Pratschs and their eldest daughter, Mrs. Darling.

The family in 1885 numbered seven, requiring them to build an eight-room wood-frame house in Aberdeen at the corner of Wishkah and F streets. They quickly entered the commercial community, the ensuing boom eventually forcing them into the hotel business. The Pratsch home became an informal restaurant run by Mrs. Pratsch for transient loggers and fishermen, rapidly becoming formalized into a restaurant providing home-cooked meals for over two hundred patrons a day.

As the town prospered, the inadequacies of its only hotel caused leading businessmen in 1889 to propose that C. A. Pratsch enlarge his home into a second badly needed hotel. He agreed, and a new building named The Pioneer House was quickly built across the street from their original house. Charles Robert, a stalwart thirty-two-year-old, built a great deal of the hotel himself. It was difficult construction, as it was built on wooden pilings driven into the Chehalis tideflats. The hotel's lively motion at high tide was rarely forgotten by its guests.

Even though the hotel required wood stoves to heat it and kerosene lamps to light it, it became the social and political center of the little village in short order. It was a site for church services, dances, funeral orations, lectures, and marriages. Politics were discussed there, and it housed the town's post office as well, presided over by the hotel proprietor, Charles August Pratsch. A stanch Democrat, he had been appointed to the post in 1886 by the first Cleveland administration. He served the community for three years, surrendering the post in 1889.

Mrs. Willard Long, a surviving family member, recalls in a letter: "When C. A. Pratsch became ill and bedfast, Mrs. Pratsch took over the business of running the hotel, she milked the cows morning and night, done all the cooking, all the baking. She baked all the cookies, cakes and pies . . . stirred everything by hand . . . 12 loaves of bread at a time. She also made soap, candles, prepared *all* the food and helped serve the meals. Through it all she kept a wonderful sense of humor."

The old hotel was enlarged by successive additions over the years, and changed its name to the Del Monte House. It luckily survived the great fire of 1903, was finally sold by the Pratsches in 1917, and was badly burned and partially destroyed in August 1919.

In addition to the hotel, the family built a bakery and confectionery, calling it Mrs. Pratsch and Co. They were all kept busy, there was work for all. For some there were full-time jobs; for others, such as Charles Robert, it was a random responsibility. He was not devoted to hotel work, and he seized the opportunity in 1885–86 to learn photography.

He paid three hundred dollars to a professional photographer from Spokane and Seattle, a Mr. Tolman or Tollman, either Jesse W. or Thomas W., to teach him how to make negatives and prints. Mr. Tolman and his wife, Emily, a photographic retoucher, operated at that time at several locations in the Pacific Northwest. Pratsch learned well enough and quickly enough so that he formed a partnership with Tolman to run a photographic studio in Aberdeen. Surviving mounted prints bearing the names Tolman and Pratsch verify the association, although it was dissolved in 1888 when Tolman and his wife left Aberdeen for California. Seizing the chance to see California, Pratsch accompanied the Tolmans and made a few landscape negatives on the journey that survive today.

In Aberdeen his studio, called The Art Gallery, was in the 200 block of F street. Both the gallery entrance and the "printing window" needed to print his negatives by natural light opened on F street. He purchased needed supplies from Woodward and Clark, photographic wholesalers in Portland. His wife, Mary Borden Pratsch, assisted in the studio and darkroom in many ways. She made a great many of his prints, mounted and burnished them on a series of heated rollers he contrived, and took charge of such bookkeeping and billing services as were needed. It is astonishing that this tiny backwoods studio owned fifty printing frames.

Pratsch shared his enthusiasm for photography with a young Canadian logger, Colin S. McKenzie. So badly injured by a falling building in the Aberdeen fire of 1903 that he was unable to continue to make his living as a logger, McKenzie appealed to Pratsch to teach him the craft. Pratsch obliged, loaning him a small gallery near his own in the building across from The Pioneer House, as well as allowing him free use of his equipment. McKenzie secured a stamp machine which allowed him to make multiple portrait images on one sheet of photographic printing paper. These could then be cut out individually and made up into salable "buttons," a popular form of photographic portraiture. Profits from this enterprise enabled young McKenzie to start up in business as a photographer in Aberdeen.

Although Pratsch and McKenzie were close, they were never partners. McKenzie worked independently until his tragic death in 1912 when he was shot by John Tournow, whom he had been trailing as a deputy-sheriff member of a hastily organized posse. After his death all his negatives, prints, and equipment were given to Pratsch.

Pratsch himself died in 1937 at the age of eighty, a few days after walking into a slowly moving train.

Everything we know about him suggests that he wanted to be a businessman making his living as a professional photographer. His still surviving cameras and the studio furnishings we can glimpse in his portraits were all of professional caliber. As final evidence, the photographs he made are professional in appearance and quality.

If he did make his living selling pictures in Aberdeen, who bought them? There were always some customers for photographs in the little sawmilling towns, of course. It was fashionable for businessmen and merchants—mill owners and ship owners in Aberdeen's case—to order photographs of their establishments, their staffs and workmen, and even a picture or two of whatever they produced for sale. Some of Pratsch's pictures are of that kind—see those of workmen, hod carriers, painters, and telephone linemen assembled on a dripping wharf under their separate trade union banners each dressed in his Sunday best. He took others: an assembled volunteer fire company; uncertain merchants standing in the doorway of their newly opened emporium; the set-portrait piece, three generations of a proud family; the local Knights of Pythias in uniformed splendor. Bread-and-butter pictures they are, the kind one would expect his customers would be happy to buy, the run-of-the-mill pictures he would take to earn his living.

Saloonkeepers would sometimes buy a photograph or two to decorate the space behind their bars. Proud loggers grouped around their new donkey engine was a popular image. Shipmasters in their pride would sometimes purchase a portrait of the ship they commanded, but not too many other people would spend their hard-earned cash on pictures—maybe a portrait to send back home, but nothing else. Not in those tough days in Washington Territory.

Two points of circumstantial evidence support the belief that he sold few pictures.

First, almost no example of his work has shown up mounted, as was customary by a professionsl photographer, on a cardboard mount imprinted with the artist's name. Second, none of his prints are to be found in major collections of Washington photographs, such as at the University of Washington and the Washington State Historical Society.

Most people in the tidewater towns of Grays Harbor were not yet so sophisticated as to indulge their taste for the finer things of life with bound albums of photographs of Indians, loggers, ships, and trees displayed in their living rooms. Looking at the Pratsch photographs of some of the cabins of the loggers and stump ranchers, one imagines they were lucky if they had a single room, let alone a living room. These pictures of Grays Harbor frontier life could not have been of great interest to most of Aberdeen's and Hoquiam's citizens, particularly if they had to pay for them. To outsiders, perhaps, they were of even less concern. Look at them! The subjects are usually no more important than the local football team, the town band, the ungainly hotel that failed on Hoquiam's tideflats, the slimy fish wharf on a frosty morning, a newly built wooden boardwalk disappearing into the nearby thick forest. Who wanted such pictures, who wanted to spend money to buy them? Why would anyone want to keep them, to say nothing of the money and energy needed to take them in the first place?

One answer may be that the photographer, Charles Robert Pratsch, Aberdeenian almost since its founding, wanted these pictures as a record he could cherish and share, images of the growth of the town to which he had given his affection. He would not have been the first. Other frontier photographers had done exactly that before him.

His photographs imply the intensity of affection and pride the townspeople and the photographer shared in the evidence all about them of their accomplishments. They had after all carved their homes and their livelihoods out of the gloomy Northwest forests. They had come to an inhospitable land with little but their energies and their determination, stuck it out, and triumphed. They had transformed the wilderness in which they had chosen to live.

The town and its day-to-day activities were living proof for them that their dream of America was becoming a reality. The hopes and aspirations they shared were coming true. If not all of them, then some of them, and if not now, then little by little. Nothing could dim in their minds the glory of what they had done. They were proud, and Charles Pratsch, their neighbor, felt no less proud than they.

Each newly painted structure was another reminder of what they were building, another event to be celebrated and remembered. For the men, women, and children of the towns, each new store, every addition to the local hotel, each new planked sidewalk over the reeking tidal flats marked progress. A circus arriving in town, possibly the first circus many townspeople had ever seen, was a momentous event well worth being photographed. Charles Pratsch knew it was, and photographed the scene reproduced here sharing his neighbor's joy. Who would ordinarily waste a negative on so prosaic a task as testing firehoses? No one, of course, except those living in wooden towns like Aberdeen, who had more than once experienced the blazing terror of a holocaust. Our photographer knew that the images of their daily lives would interest his fellow townsmen. He knew what events animated their lives and made them memorable. He was their neighbor sharing many of their dreams, triumphs, and disappointments. If he found out that he could not make a living selling these photographs, no matter, he would pay his bills in other ways. He may have sensed the historical importance of the photographic record he was creating.

There are far too few nineteenth-century villages and towns in the United States whose growth has been recorded in photographs. Aberdeen and Hoquiam were lucky —their cameraman knew his business well. His images reveal not only what the eye can see readily on the surface, but they provide a feeling of the area, a sense of the gray overcast, the perpetual dampness that marks this wet wilderness. What C. R. Pratsch chose to photograph was true to him and true to his time, certainly for the fleeting instant it took to make an exposure. He was a faithful witness and perhaps a loving one, and we can turn to his photographs with confidence that we are seeing the Grays Harbor towns as he and his camera saw them in his day.

Hoquiam looking south across its twisting river in 1885 was not very impressive. Its pitifully small collection of homes, farms, sawmills, and churches were grim symbols of its pioneers' determination to survive in the forests. In the center of *the photograph the ship Seminole, a medium clipper in its heyday, is having its damaged fore lowermast hauled out for replacement.*

Left: *Newly organized as a town in 1885, Aberdeen was little more than a clearing in the forests that surrounded it, each of its settlers struggling to make a living. At left, to the south, the muddy Chehalis River winds its way westward, downriver, to the sea. Bisecting the city-to-be is the Wishkah River in the foreground, its east bank a future home for its first sawmills.*

Above: *The desperately needed railroad came to Hoquiam over the Chehalis River's dreary tideflats. Almost hidden behind a clump of trees at center stands the ill-fated Hoquiam Hotel, a real estate speculator's failed dream.*

It required courage, patience, and a long view of history to visualize this rugged terrain as one of Grays Harbor's main streets. In order to become Broadway, this wilderness of stumps had first to be cleared and leveled, covered with brush, spread with sawdust from the mills, and finally planked over with wide lengths of prime Douglas fir. ▶

Grays Harbor.— Broadway looking e...

from Satsop Ave. August 19, 1889.

In 1890 Wishkah Street in Aberdeen ran east to the river's edge at F Street taking its name from the narrow river. The town's structures were built on pilings out over the Chehalis tideflats to cut down on their rocking when the flooding tides were high.

The Walter L. Main Traveling Circus headed into Aberdeen in 1895 over the Wishkah River via the Heron Street Bridge. Their entrance went well until the elephants, frightened by the vibrations of the bridge's wooden planks, balked at the crossing. Only the coaxing of the circus employees brought the trembling beasts down F street safely as shown here. Parading down the street between Wishkah and Heron, the circus attracts the attention of every lounger and most of the merchants, even young Wallace Pratsch riding his tricycle in front of his photographer father's Art Gallery.

Few of Grays Harbor's settlers overlooked the Fourth of July in Aberdeen in 1892. As they assembled to give thanks for their freedoms, the town center, Heron and G streets, was almost choked with flags and red, white, and blue bunting. The forested hills to the west, as yet uncut, loom over the town, the still unplanked forest floor stretching east to the banks of the Wishkah River.

Aberdeen's Barbary Coast, Heron and F, the infamous "Line." Here in 1892 some men sinned in grimy splendor while others profited handsomely. Luminescent in gaudy pleasure, liquid and otherwise, this grubby street was a sailors' and loggers' sinful heaven on earth. Quiet by day, lurid by night, it housed more saloons, brothels, cheap-jack tailor stores, thieves, con men, and assorted rascals than the town's fathers wished to have known. This short dirt street was notorious in every major seaport of the world.

Left: *Aberdeen grew without much planning, wandering over its low hills to the north and west. Cleared of its trees by 1907, the land attracted new investors. Neighbors now lived closer to one another, the old open spaces and former loneliness gone forever. Almost everyone still depended for good fortune on lumber. Piled in profusion here on the mill docks for sea shipment, the sawn lumber symbolizes their ongoing prosperity.*

Above: *The horror of fire in a closely packed town built entirely of wood is indescribable. In 1903 such a tragedy devastated large sections of downtown Aberdeen. The panic and helplessness that infect many at such a time are vivid in this picture taken after the 1903 holocaust.*

*Only a fantasy to create a pop-
ular beach resort on the
Chehalis mud at Hoquiam could
have given birth to this rambling
white elephant. A local monument to greed and poor judg-
ment, this seaside hotel was
built a half mile from water at
low tide by optimists envision-
ing wealth from tourists the
railroad was expected to bring
to the harbor. It never managed
to pay its way.*

Aberdeen's wooden high school in 1892 was a monument to the art of fancy millwork with its sawn ornamental wooden shapes. Standing on one of the town's higher hills, it almost shouted parents' determination that their children get an education, the road they believed led to success in this new world.

Below: *A temple of the Lord at the forest's green door, Aberdeen's Methodist Church stands in lonely isolation at First and F streets. Its only neighbor, a single house on the hill behind it, belongs to Aberdeen's patriarch founder, Samuel Benn.*

Opposite: *Every new building completed was hailed in the town's forming years, even an inflammable structure such as this splendidly painted example housing the Aberdeen Post Office in 1890. It is cunningly located next door to the town's sole stationery establishment.*

Opposite: Standing ready for customers, this newly opened grocery store, still bordered by wood-planked streets and planked wooden sidewalks, is among the first brick buildings thrown up to replace Aberdeen's many wooden firetraps. Only a succession of devastating fires finally banned wood construction in the town's center.

Below: In Catherine Pratsch's new store on Heron street with its stock imported from nearby Portland and Seattle, shopping was often a journey of discovery into a new and fascinating world for many Aberdeenians isolated in the harbor's tiny mill towns. The local postmaster, Charles A. Pratsch, framed in the post office wicket at the store's rear, peers out ready to serve.

Perhaps such family portraits of Grays Harbor pioneers, at least those who had prospered, were photographer Pratsch's bread-and-butter work. Taken in his tiny Art Gallery on F street, this print reveals familiar posing props which appear in other of his portrait studies.

The Pratsch clan in 1888, four years after their arrival at Grays Harbor. Seated from left to right are: Carrie Clara Pratsch; Charles August Pratsch and Catherine Anna Pratsch, the photographer's father and mother; and Emma Ida Pratsch. Standing left to right: Charles Robert Pratsch, the photographer; Margaret Mae Pratsch, Laura Bessie Pratsch, Catherine Hannah Pratsch, and Frank Seigle Pratsch.

Opposite: Staring bleakly into a rapidly changing community, Charles August Pratsch, nearing the end of his life, evidences the strains he endured.

Opposite: *A self-confident young man, secure in his youthful vigor, the photographer C. R. Pratsch sits for a self-portrait.*

The photographer's mother, the remarkable Catherine Anna Pratsch—good-natured, devoted to her family, and hard-working beyond belief.

Dressed for a portrait in her Sunday finery, one of the photographer's sisters, Carrie Clara Pratsch, musters up only the faintest sweet smile, perhaps to her brother's repeated urging to "say cheese and show teeth."

The nineteenth-century tea party as a fit subject for photographic clichés was not confined to the grand galleries and studios of New York and San Francisco. Clear proof that "la bonne vie" was much admired in backwoods Aberdeen is offered here by photographer Pratsch.

Unknown gentlemen sitting for their photographs in those formal days could pose only in dead-serious solemnity. The long exposures required by the glass plates made candid photography impossible.

Organized into Local No. 146 of the International Hod Carriers and Bricklayers Union of America, these assembled Aberdeen proletarians stand proud in their uniforms, their badges, and their hard-won independence.

A gallery of Aberdeen's laboring trade unionists.

Although any hook-and-ladder truck was theoretically equipped to do everything needed to contain a fire, in fact it often proved inadequate. In a town built almost completely of wood, this classic example, Aberdeen's pride, proved no less so.

A formal view of Aberdeen's hand-pumpers surrounded by the brawn and stamina needed to keep them functioning. Such volunteer fire groups, while strong in zeal and enthusiastic in performance, were never a satisfactory answer to Aberdeen's ever-present fire danger.

Opposite: Testing the town's fire hoses was an event celebrated by the young as a festival organized for their special diversion. Spouting streams of river water high in the air, the hoses transformed any normal day into an exciting circus for Aberdeen's children.

Above: Among the proud fishermen, amateurs all, are some of Aberdeen's young stalwarts: from left to right, Fred Hewitt, Ernie Phelps, Johnny McCook, and Colin S. McKenzie, our woods photographer. It is doubtful that legal limits for fish were in force at that time if this abundance is any example.

Left: Providing fish for Aberdeen's canneries was a full-time occupation for its fishermen. Fresh-caught sturgeon lie on the fish dock, the curious children examining the wonder of fish out of water, puzzled over why such a prosaic scene is worth recording for posterity.

Unbowed by the heavy load of ducks around his middle, this level-eyed hunter greets the camera with the same sharp eye that aimed his shotgun so successfully.

Happy in their new uniforms, nose guards, leg guards, and padded pants, the 1907 high-school eleven pose in manly sobriety.

The proud Aberdeen High School football team in 1905, an accepted example of sturdy manhood.

Opposite: *No less proud, the basketball stalwarts of Aberdeen High School in 1907.*

*Each member of Aberdeen's
1890 Square Deal Baseball
Club, from player to mustachi-
oed manager, bears the town's
honor on his shoulders.*

Aberdeen's sandlot ball park, home of the city ball team, in 1907.

Opposite: *Two noted Aberdeenians at a Fourth of July log-bucking contest. The winner, the famous shipmaster Matt Peasley on the left, and in the center, holding the saw, notorious Billy Gohl, Aberdeen's infamous mass murderer, trying to share Peasley's moment of fame.*

Below: *Man's best friend on Grays Harbor was often his boat or his horse, perhaps his ox or his cow, rather than his dog. Powerful draft horses, faithful helpers around a farm, were eagerly sought and highly prized by their owners. Livery stables and competent teamsters abounded in Grays Harbor, and handling horses was a skill accorded considerable esteem.*

Their tinsel somewhat tarnished in the glare of day, the bartenders, bouncers, and "girls" of Ed Dolan's Eagle Dance Hall and Casino line up for posterity.

Ready to provide the rowdy entertainment their customers expected, the Casino staff were a rough crowd who served doped drinks, rolled drunks, and shanghaied many an innocent visitor.

Strictly a men's sanctuary, this social club offered its customers pool, whiskey, smoking, and highly colored pictures of near-naked women.

The high life of Aberdeen's "Line" included the Lone Jack Saloon. Furnished rooms upstairs were equipped with female companions for rent by the hour . . . and the watchword was, watch your wallet!

Opposite top: *As elsewhere in nineteenth-century United States, the Old-World love of uniforms and pomp lived on in Aberdeen. Among the more celebrated members of Aberdeen's Knights Templars were the famed deep-water Master, Matt Peasley, standing in the top row, right, and the well-known skipper of the tug Traveler, "Draw-Bucket" Johnson, second from left in the second row.*

Opposite bottom: *Many Grays Harbor citizens played instruments quite well, and in each of the harbor towns local brass bands were formed. This ensemble has gathered for practice on the broad steps of Hoquiam's ill-fated hotel.*

Old-soldier members of the Grand Army of the Republic celebrate at their grounds near the beach at Westport, aided by the City Band of Aberdeen. Only twenty-five years after the Civil War's end the participants' memories are still keen, and free beer and free lies are exchanged with laughing impunity.

Left: Few reasons were needed to picnic on the harbor; finding the time for such recreation was always the problem. This gathering is made up largely of children, women, and older men. Most able-bodied men were at work.

Above: Weary holidaygoers at the beach hustle along Westport's creaking wharf hoping not to miss the river steamers assembled to carry them home. Each of them, the Clan McDonald, City of Aberdeen, Typhoon, and Chehalis, flies the flag in celebration of the Fourth of July.

A stellar attraction on the beach in 1892 was young Harry Perkins on his high-wheel bicycle. There were no amusement parks then, and neighbors depended on one another for their diversion, even young Fred Pratsch, aged two, in the group at the right. ►

The lumber schooner Nora Harkins, freshly stranded, is still her owner's concern. The sailors aboard her unbend the mainsail for use another day, perhaps in another vessel if the Harkins is not gotten off the beach.

*Firmly bedded on the beach,
the Nora Harkins, abandoned
and ravaged, is useful now only
for sightseers, her bowsprit a
dependable perch from which
to rig a primitive swing.*

Below: *Whatever roads traversed the harbor in its founding days were planked roads, leading in and out of the forests through the clearings, linking the tiny mill towns together like beads on a necklace. This one leading into Montesano is typical, wide enough for a horse-and-carriage or two cyclists riding abreast.*

Opposite: *The adventurous could ride the planked road from Hoquiam to the Pacific beaches in 1893, and young Manning Hills could not wait to try out his brand-new high-wheeler just arrived from a mail-order house in Chicago.*

Even then a pretty woman or two, a dog, and the great outdoors were unbeatable subjects for photographers. Grays Harbor was well provided with each and with enough amateur photographers to make good use of them.

Even though wet, gloomy, and riddled with shattered tree stumps, the nearby forest proved a romantic spot for many young lovers and some few older ones, including the aptly posed "Dying Gladiator" in the foreground.

Opposite: Two rugged choppers, transformed through the courtesy of a mail-order house from the rough-looking hoboes they appear to be at their work, stand proudly in the environment they know best, the wet woods. No Eastern city dandy ever looked more proper, and our heroes pose for their portraits as though they know it.

The appeal of a junk shop was hard to resist even in backwoods Aberdeen. A failed business might provide a convenient location, another the merchandise required. For many customers this mill-town antique shop often proved a temple of opportunity, not unlike a present-day garage sale.

Motorcycles, hunting skiffs, rifles, shotguns, even bayoneted muskets were each important requirements for living at Grays Harbor. They dominate the stock at Aberdeen's most successful sporting goods establishment.

Displays of domestic affluence were far from common in harbor homes, but this well-furnished living room of Jesse O. Stearns, one of our photographers, a first-rate amateur, is explained by his vocation as vice-president of the Hoquiam bank.

Opposite top: Posing for an informal portrait, these Hoquiam citizens, quarantined in their homes by smallpox, take a much-needed breath of fresh air in front of the photographer's camera.

Opposite bottom: Transient fishermen and loggers comprised the majority of the guests at the Riverside Hotel. They and the hotel's chambermaids, assembled on the verandah for this photograph, pose in working-class solemnity. Custom and prejudice demanded that on such occasions the sexes be chastely separated.

Alone in the dark woods, hemmed in by giant trees, the homes of these hard-working "stump ranch" families are a reminder of the labor and determination needed to endure in Washington's wet wilderness. In the beginning, most of the houses were makeshift and meager, although the mill-sawn siding that decorates the front of one of them is evidence of its owner's relative success.

Hard by the rugged forest, Aberdeen's citizens share an outdoor service in front of their church, their tiny ones looking on. The newly erected pastor's house is at right.

Any loss in the harbor's small communities was deeply felt, and the number of mourners in attendance here is ample evidence. For the dead in 1888 an upriver voyage to the Fern Cemetery on one of Aberdeen's steamboats, the Josie Burrows or the Toiwo, was a must, for only there was ground dry enough to guarantee the dead a secure burial.

The Dark Woods

The cry of "Tim-berrr" has echoed through the nation's forests from the first day its colonists searched the woods for lumber to build their homes. Many Eastern settlers moved on to the West, felling trees for their sawmills as they went. Having nearly denuded Maine's abundant forests by the 1850s, they left those of Michigan and Wisconsin almost depleted in the 1890s, and by the 1900s lumber-barons-to-be and loggers alike had invaded California, Oregon, and Washington is search of even more abundant forests. They came with sharpened axes in their hands, ready to cut down whatever trees stood in their paths. The West, they knew, was the last great area of standing trees, for they had already cut down every forest they had walked through. Behind them lay barren timberland. They came looking to buy whatever land had trees ready for sawmilling, and for many a day in the Pacific Northwest, almost *anywhere* fitted that description.

Every kind of lumberman—Scandinavians, Scots, Frenchmen, and State of Mainers—came West to cut lumber, but at their shoulders stood other men with money looking for opportunities to invest. Formed into powerful syndicates, they knew a good thing when they saw it, and they invested their money in the promising land and tall trees of the Pacific Northwest. The Northern Pacific Railway and Jim Hill's Great Northern, both driving West, were crisscrossing the land to their Pacific Ocean terminuses, one to Seattle, the other to Tacoma. The forested lands they opened up were "green gold" waiting only to be felled and sawn into money, a trick that required mainly cheap labor, quick sawmilling, and speedy transport to world markets. Big

The endless Washington forests were dark, dense, and valuable, holding the greatest stands of Douglas fir in the entire Pacific Northwest. Settled first by disappointed gold seekers from the California Rush, the area next was host to brawny European immigrants from the forests of Michigan and Wisconsin. They were skilled and determined men— hard-working aliens in a strange land who came to lumber in hope of finding a better life in the United States.

money, wisely invested, could accomplish miracles. Investors did not wait, they moved quickly into the new territories, cornering the best timberlands, the thickest forests, and the most suitable locations in the new towns. What with the lands secured by the railway interests as rights of way and the timberlands owned by investment syndicates, little was left for later arrivals. The combined power of the monied interests settled the destiny of the new territory for a long time into the future. Effective economic control of the vast area was no longer up for grabs as many people thought—a crucial fact of life most settlers took a long time to recognize. For some, this crushing reality was never too clear, and they suffered cruelly for their ignorance and naiveté.

The first lumbering methods imported by Eastern loggers were the ancient ways. Pioneer Western loggers used the double-bitted axe, the hand-screw jack, the two-handed crosscut saw, the ox team, the whiskey keg, the skill and experience of old loggers, and, finally, the determination and endurance to fell trees that had proved so devastating to the decimated forests in the East. The loggers quickly cut a swath through the new timber stands, leveling each tree they could touch, felling it wherever it stood. The only form of power in the dark woods at that time was no more than the combined muscle power of oxen, men, and the simplest of stout levers. For years this power alone had brought great trees down to the forest floor. Once the tree was on the ground, heavy chains were shackled around its trunk, often at great danger to the youngsters who crawled under the fallen tree to complete the task. Teams of six to eight oxen yoked together were hitched to the readied tree and urged on by endless blasphemies, steady prodding in their flanks, and the assistance of greased skid roads buried in the forest floor. The great logs were simply dragged by the straining beasts to the nearest flowing streams. Such available fast water would quickly carry the logs to tidewater sawmills waiting to cut them up into salable lumber.

These old-fashioned methods served lumbermen well enough until a simple piece of nineteenth-century contrivance, a mechanical animal stronger than any ox, the donkey engine, transformed the whole business of getting trees out of the woods. A clever woods mechanic, John Dolbeer, down on Humboldt Bay among the California redwoods, invented the puffing beast, this donkey engine. He made his name immortal among lumbermen and got rich in the bargain. In a game like logging, involving the directed movement of tons of logs over hilly slopes, *sustained power* was needed, more power than men and animals had ever produced. Steam won out over manpower. It was steam power, finally, James Watt's brilliant contribution to man's flight from servitude, that offered the needed answer. The steam donkey proved extremely effective the first time it was used in the woods. With its use in the tall timber, a revolution in logging was successfully imported from California into the Northwest woods.

With steam pressure available from an upright donkey boiler mounted on wooden skids and harnessed to a vertical spool—a capstan that could reel in steel wire wound upon a drum or let it out at the flick of an engineer's hand—the woods were mechanized. The donkey engine shattered long-hallowed precedents, and the old days were over almost in an instant, at least no longer than it took a logging company to purchase the new equipment. No more the inspired profanity of the bullwhacker urging on his straining oxen. No more the grunts and bellows of dumb beasts driven beyond their limits. Paul Bunyan and Babe, his blue ox, stank of steam now. The few logs per day formerly produced by a crew of strong men using axes and saws, hard-breathing oxen, hemp rope, and chains quickly became a tale lost in memory.

The price for such improvement proved murderous, for now the woods were clever traps of steel wire, taut and dangerous cat's cradles wickedly concealed in thick underbrush. Laced with cunning skill from the donkey spool through great steel blocks and back again to the donkey engine, such mazes of wire transformed the woods into shrieking centers of mechanical wizardry. It seemed Dante's Inferno come to life. The woods seemed alive with puffing engines shrouded in smoke and steam, groaning trees crashing to the forest floor, and saws whining and howling amidst the shouts of loggers intent on their mad work. Tree trunks were dragged through the forest by the new donkey engines as though they were small stones or pebbles shot from oversized slingshots. Formerly the old-time logger had only to keep clear of falling trees and branches; now there were whipping steel wires that cut men in two as though they were butter. Logs were whipped through the underbrush at express-train speed, crushing anything that stood in their path. Nothing was sacred except production; warnings were not expected, and few were given. That was the new way. And so, deep in Washington's forest of Douglas fir, red cedar, spruce, and hemlock, lost among California's giant redwoods, the ancient timber business was transformed into an even bigger business. First, there was steam power to replace oxen and men; then electricity in all its amazing adaptations; and finally the speeded-up requirements of mass production, which changed the methods and attitudes of the old-time lumbermen forever.

Even as these drastic changes greatly altered the way men got lumber out of the forests, the conditions in which the loggers lived and died were little changed from the old days. They still lived together deep in the gloomy woods in ill-lit, shabby wooden bunkhouses, mere shacks standing cheek by jowl alongside the tree stumps. Their isolation from nearby towns was still as complete as ever, their only company being the crews of the logging trains whose routes ran through their camps, their visiting supervisors, a stray timber cruiser (a woodsman employed by a lumber company to roam the woods to locate trees suitable for cutting down), wandering oxen, and each other. Their food was coarse and plentiful, the kind they needed in order to work as hard and long as they did.

The photographs of these forest dwellers can help us understand how intensely they worked, even though such back-breaking labor will appear strange to us. They seem to be young and enduring—at least many of them do; daring to be otherwise in the woods was too risky and too grueling. These grimy-looking men were not pretty; they couldn't be. They dressed no better than their work required. The woods were no place for fashion plates; tin pants (hard-wearing denims), husky boots, and a pair of lived-in B.V.D.s were the height of style for a working logger. They had earned the right to be tired. Swing a heavy, double-bitted axe for hours, and then push and pull a two-man saw—"a misery whip"—to strain already weary muscles, and you have the picture.

There was no identity crisis among these men. They knew who they were and what they did for a living. See how they stand with firm grace on their springboards high above the underbrush below them. They ready the huge tree with undercutting axes, planning the tree's fall to land it on the forest floor, undamaged, where they had prepared its coming. Everyone understood that damaged trunks made no money. The skill and endurance of these choppers were fabled. A hallowed response to their abilities is summed up in the well-known retort, "The men who cut down that tree are damned liars."

For the choppers, merely to live in the woods was to be in danger. Fully aware of the forest's many hazards, remembering that heedless men in the woods died early, they labored hard, backs bent to demanding saws, but always in tension, alert to every shouted warning call or any strange noise, which they dared not ignore.

As their labor was brutal, their release from its tensions was equally rough and vigorous. The loggers' roughhouse play in the saloons and bordellos of Grays Harbor's Barbary Coast was often so frightening in its competitive savagery, mirroring the violence of their trade, that many onlookers turned away in horror. Fist fights were common, and there were no rules; eye gouging, knees to groins, stamping with caulked boots on unconscious opponents—anything went. Hurling one another across a barroom or out of a second-story brothel window frequently resulted in crippling injuries and even death. Seafaring men, no angels in their own relaxation, visiting Grays Harbor for the first time, usually stood aside from the loggers' revels, in shocked awe at their ferocity.

While the lumbermen often came to the Washington woods with the hope of reaping sudden wealth, another group came with more modest ambitions. These were the farmers, most of them European immigrants anxious to own and farm their own land, determined to become independent, no longer debt-ridden and class-bound peasants of Old Country memory. The thick woods proved a formidable obstacle to them, even though many had managed successfully in the early days, the 1850s, 60s, and 70s. Their small farms dotted many stumpy clearings. The forest demanded a high price for cleared land; it always had. No land anywhere could be farmed until it had been cleared of trees, stumps, and rocks; every farmer knew that. It was no different in southwestern Washington, only harder. Here were no gently swelling hills as in Nebraska or flat Kansas prairies for easy farming. First, the great trees had to be felled and then dragged off the intended fields. The labor involved in wrestling the remaining stumps can be better imagined than described. They broke some men's will and their backs as well. It is not surprising to see in these photographs pictures of the "first home," usually a pitiful shack, deep in a shadowed clearing, almost cowering under towering firs. So common was it for early farmers to plow up to and around still-standing tree stumps, lumps of wood too deeply rooted and too massive and heavy to uproot at all, that the farmers were disdainfully called "stump ranchers." Southwestern Washington stump ranchers were obliged to spread their fields in the shadows of the tallest trees most men had ever seen.

The great trees were a minor blessing of sorts. In the early days, it paid any farmer clearing his land to get the trees he had to cut anyway downstream to a sawmill. Any stream dammed to build up water pressure could be counted on when its water was released to carry the logs backed up behind it to the mill at tidewater. The pay to the farmer was not much, about fifty cents per tree in the early days, but it turned out to be found money at a time when every cent of cash counted greatly. For the sawmill operator, sometimes a failed farmer who could not afford to send a team of loggers into the woods to fell trees for his mill, the tiny clutches of such logs were a godsend.

Between them, the stubborn farmers and the lumbermen did much to make the Grays Harbor wilderness passable. They both needed roads to get in and out of the woods, to haul supplies, and, for the loggers most of all, to get out the logs. Roads were the central question for everyone. For the farmer, roads meant contact with neighboring towns, as in the case of Aberdeen and Hoquiam, separated in the beginning by three miles of dense forest. Clearing meant new tillable ground, and it was warmly welcomed, even if a farmer himself had to clear the slash left by the lumbermen.

For the lumberman, communication with the tiny towns, the sawmills in particular, was vital. Without it, loggers were useless in the woods. It did not matter how crude the roads were—anything on the order of a road would serve their needs. Where they were needed, the lumbermen built ox trails through the woods or "skid roads," made of greased logs half buried in the forest floor, over which they skidded the trees they had cut down. Many of the later paved highways and major dirt roads were laid down where the early roads had been cut originally.

As the lumber business changed, the woods changed. In time remarkable methods would come for getting felled trees out of the forest using high leads, spar trees, aerial tramways, even helicopters, but their day was still far in the future. For our photographers, Charles Robert Pratsch and his logger colleague Colin McKenzie, the ancient way, long practiced and well understood, was the logging they knew best, the way of logging they had always lived with and the one they were most at home photographing in the dim forests, surrounded by dust, noise, and danger.

Clearing these dark woods for tillable land was brutal work, interminable and punishing. The Guffeys, Fred Honley's neighbors at Wishkah Falls, lived cheek by jowl with the remnants of the trees they had cut to clear the land. Far too deeply rooted to be easily wrenched from the forest floor by any one man or even two, the stumps' ugly presence had to be tolerated.

The tallest trees most men had ever seen shadowed the gloomy forests near Fred Honley's stump ranch at Wishkah Falls, making his visitors, tall men, seem like pygmies.

*The pitiful ranches were no vi-
sion of delight. They provided
little more than shelter for bone-
weary settlers and a hope that
the better life they sought might
be found here in the dark
Washington woods.*

Wherever man-made structures were found in the forest, each bore the marks of fresh-sawn lumber, often by hand saw. Some buildings were flimsy and temporary, while others were placed on the earth to last, as was this Borden family ranch house at Wishkah Falls in 1892.

Loggers' camps were the loneliest outposts in the forest, rough and profane at their best. A child or two at a camp transformed the men into models of virtue and kindness. Youngsters could count on endless adoration and hand-carved toys in profusion. At Wilson's Camp (below, right) the cookhouse labor was done by women, too few for the work, helped by any children old enough to fetch and carry. The loggers came, ate quickly, said "Thank you, Ma'am," and returned immediately to the woods. The busy cookhouse of the Flowers Camp (below) was a form of community center, a makeshift meeting place. In addition to ample quantities of home-cooked food, badly needed companionship was offered each day at mealtime.

Below: *Labor in the forests was dirty, wet, and grueling and, by today's standards, poorly paid. The brush was tangled and slippery, mosquitoes were everywhere, and the oxen seemed stupid and rebellious, yet the loggers, working like Trojans, gloried in each other's success. Opposite: The choppers faced their quarry, towering eighty feet or more above their heads, with only two double-bitted axes, a two-handed crosscut saw, a bottle of kerosene to keep the saw from sticking in the wet wood, a few metal wedges, a small maul, and the certain knowledge that ultimate victory would be theirs. Standing on narrow springboards, they undercut the trunks with razor-sharp axes while the crosscut saw, the "misery whip," awaited its labors, to be eased in its way through the wood by the lubricating kerosene. In the final scene, the choppers in a forest near the Johns River on Grays Harbor's south shore in 1888 have finished their skilled work. Soon the saw, already in place in the cut, will bring the forest giant down.*

The Clark and Mills woods crew of choppers, buckers, and choke setters pose for young Colin McKenzie, who had been a logger like themselves before he became a woods photographer.

The enduring men who felled the great trees knew both exultation in accomplishment and the simple exhaustion that was so much a part of their daily, wearying triumphs.

PHOTO BY MACKENZIE

Choppers, buckers, mule skinners, and their straining oxen such as these stalwarts from Gil Skeen's Camp in 1888 were a team, united in their efforts. They had to be. It was the only way their puny muscle power could be marshaled against their quarry, the great trees.

Opposite top: *Half buried in the forest floor, and well greased ahead of ox teams dragging fallen tree trunks to waiting streams, the skid road, a relic of older logging days, was used until replaced by snorting donkey engines. Working out of George Keith's Camp in 1889, hand loggers still relied on the "skid" to move logs out of the woods.*

Opposite bottom: *After loggers passed through the forest felling everything they could get an axe into, clearings looked as though a troop of mad giants had rushed through kicking down whatever stood in their path. The waste of the trees in those days was frightful and unnecessary.*

When a lumber company woods office moved from one cutting area to another where it was newly needed, it was rebuilt each time as little more than a shack. Timber cruisers and woods bosses gather at one here.

A typical view of a donkey engine and its crew deep in Grays Harbor's wet, gloomy woods. Although each of these tough loggers is able and experienced, they are no match for the ear-splitting power of steam under pressure, a fact they have accepted quickly. Backed up by their mechanical ox, they have few doubts about their mastery over nature.

Opposite: Donkey crews looked like hoboes, but they were not. Their work was hard and dirty, and loggers dressed for the part, and only a darn fool would shave with cold water each day. Who, after all, needed to impress anyone in the woods?

A donkey engine didn't look like much, and when it wasn't working, it didn't sound impressive either, panting quietly in short, soft breaths like a tired dog. But when it was going full tilt, smoking, screaming, and pulling like ten devils, it was blessed by every logger, who relied on its unbelievable power and versatility.

Securely mounted on huge logs fashioned into a crude sled, the donkey engine could be taken wherever loggers needed it. Its own power converted into a winch could do the trick easily, a remarkable spectacle to watch in the forest's close quarters. Growling, spitting fire and smoke, throwing dirt in every direction, it amazed everyone by its adaptability.

Left: *The maze of wire rope and pulleys, often concealed in the underbrush between the donkey engine and its load, was a dangerous cat's cradle. A snapped wire thrashing about like a maddened snake could deal out frightful death in an instant. It was no place for carelessness; the price in broken bodies was too great.*

Above: *Wherever fallen trees lay in the forest ready for the tidewater sawmills the donkey was brought to the job. No location proved too difficult, up-slope or downslope—it was all the same to donkey jockeys. Wood from the forest provided ready fuel, but getting enough water for the hot boiler posed a more serious problem. The weather meant little; the donkey, a mechanical beast hard to beat, worked whenever there was work to be done.*

Opposite: *Every tree snatched from the forest demanded punishing labor. If ever ingenuity was needed, the tall trees in Grays Harbor's dense woods required it. With trees in thick abundance, tangled underbrush everywhere, and open forest spaces choked with standing stumps, every type of skid road, narrow, wide, flat, or hilly, was built. From simple downhill gravity to the donkey engine's steam power, every available assist was used to get the logs out of the forests to tidewater sawmills.*

Below: *Once steam successfully invaded the forest, the logging railroad had to follow. Deep in the Grays Harbor woods, this Shay locomotive, No. 546, belonging to the A. F. Coats Lumber Company, sits for its portrait on Alex Polson's trestle over the Humptulips River. The logs chained directly to the car's trucks are an innovative solution for transporting timber by rail.*

Almost always wreathed in steam and smoke, the sawmills loomed out of the harbor's persistent fogs as great smoking devils, frightening monsters of the imagination. Groaning steam engines and howling saws at night lent substance to the illusion. No one who saw such mills as this at Hoquiam in 1888 ever forgot them.

The Hoquiam Shingle and Lumber Company, looking like a small industrial empire, dominates the wild-looking landscape. The empire nestles just inside the first bend of the Hoquiam River, overshadowing the nearby town. Its many mills, power houses, mill stores, lumber yards, and managers' homes take on the appearance of a small town in its own right.

The Ships on the Harbor

It was the most natural thing in the world for the men in Grays Harbor's little towns to build their own ships. Isolated in their tidewater communities, their businesses and livelihoods dependent on water transport, they needed ships of every kind. Without them they were virtually helpless. In the beginning they got their ships elsewhere, Portland and Seattle, for example, even though the lumber required to build the ships was literally on their own doorsteps. The remarkable Douglas fir was exactly what shipbuilders needed, and it was being cut in their own sawmills each day. It was more plentiful and cheaper in Aberdeen than buying it elsewhere and shipping it to the harbor; why not build their own ships? All they lacked to begin building was the decision, skills, and financing. These were eventually found in 1887 when Tom MacDonald built the schooner *Volunteer,* which was the start of wooden shipbuilding on Grays Harbor.

There were ships of every kind at Grays Harbor. In the Hoquiam River the four-mast schooner W. J. Patterson, built in 1901 at John Lindstrom's Aberdeen shipyard, lies ahead of the wee barkentine Gleaner, only 492 tons, built by Tom MacDonald at Hoquiam in 1892 for the Simpson mill. The popular river boat, the stern-wheeler T. C. Reed, in midstream, blows off steam as she rounds the river's last bend. Paddling downriver she makes for her ocean terminus at Westport on the harbor's south shore.

Almost anything that would float could be used, although the greatest need at first was for riverboats, steam-powered stern-wheelers. Without them, the citizens of the young towns lived in semi-isolation. Cut off from trade and overland contact by dense stands of trees, they turned to the rivers as their natural highways.

The markets for the lumber pouring out of their sawmills and for the fish from their canneries lay far to the south in San Francisco, San Pedro, and San Diego, ports that were easily reached then by oceangoing sailing vessels. Even larger ships were needed for the overseas customers for Grays Harbor lumber. The lumber-carrying ships on the Pacific Coast before the advent of steam were wooden sailing ships, schooners, brigantines, and barkentines, vessels rigged to take full advantage of the prevailing offshore winds. These were the kinds of ships they had to build at Grays Harbor, heavily built lumber carriers, not knowing that they would be replaced soon by a new breed, wooden steamships called steam schooners. They also needed to build steam tugs that could tow seagoing vessels safely past the harbor's notorious sandbars. When the tugs were not busy with the ships, they could tow log booms to waiting sawmills.

Small boats of every description, mainly fishing boats, were in great demand. Every gillnetter on the harbor wanted a boat, and many men built their own. Boat-building skills, a survival requirement on the harbor, were common in those days, and they were openly and widely shared. No man in need of a small boat to row or sail on Grays Harbor had to do without one.

Soon the harbor shipbuilders were able to build everything needed in seagoing vessels except the engines. The engines were brought to the harbor shipyards by sea from Seattle or San Francisco, though in certain cases the completed hull would be towed to larger ports where the engines could be installed and adjusted. Additionally needed skilled workers such as shipsmiths, sparmakers, sailmakers, and riggers were usually brought to the harbor shipyards in gangs, on contract, but sometimes these artisans settled there and started small businesses of their own. Ultimately, nothing was lacking in Aberdeen or Hoquiam yards to build a lumber vessel entirely from home-sawn lumber, outfit her completely, load her to the waterline or further with Grays Harbor lumber, tow her downriver to the sea behind a tugboat built in a harbor shipyard, and see her off to a profitable southbound voyage.

Shipbuilding in wood was a much-honored skill, and the artisans who worked in the yards bordering the tiny rivers, the Wishkah and the Hoquiam, were held in high esteem by the townsfolk. While rough carpenters were needed for the heavy work of framing and ceiling the ship's hull, the joiners, the much-admired craftsmen among shipwrights, were especially appreciated and were often in short supply. They were usually brawny men of great endurance, for the heavy work demanded it; the timbers used in building wooden ships have always been massive. The photographs shown of a hull in frame are vivid testimony to the size of the timbers used in abundance. Almost daily, sawn wooden beams 14″ × 14″ × 60′ were drilled to three- and four-foot depths with old-fashioned hand-driven auger bits, accurately hewn to cunning curves with broad axes and adzes, and lifted and hauled into place as needed by block, tackles, and brawn. For certain fastenings needed in assembling hulls, only treenails, long wooden dowels driven into bored holes by husky shipwrights wielding mallets, did the job properly. Where they were needed, iron ship spikes and galvanized threaded bolts were used as well. The planked hulls were caulked with tarred oakum, and the planking seams were cemented over and then painted to make the completed ship secure and dry.

The work of building ships went on each day regardless of the weather, which was mostly poor in Grays Harbor anyway. Once a ship was laid down, getting it into the water was alway a rush job. The working hours stretched from the light of a dawning day to sunset. The scene at the shipyards was often a brilliant play of light and sound marked by the dull rhythm of mallets and mauls, the fresh-sawn timber pale yellow against the gray sky. The many sounds of heavy construction dominated everything except the shrill cries of working men shouting to each other over the deafening turmoil. Green trees ringed each harbor shipyard, and a fitful sun made a silvered sheet of the river nearby; vigorous color and excitement were lent each day to otherwise prosaic labor.

No other photograph taken on the harbor more clearly reveals how much shipbuilding attracted the townsfolk's interest than the view (page 161) of the nearly finished wooden schooner *Kailua* awaiting her imminent launch. Both they and the workmen cluster around the finished hull on her ways, and in the foreground a family group sit together minding a parasol-draped baby carriage. They rest on useless timber quietly chatting, expectant, waiting to join the handclapping and shouting that will soon greet the new schooner's safe entrance into the river.

The men who organized Grays Harbor shipyards, the constructors, were master builders of proven ingenuity and dependability, recognized by ship owners up and down the Pacific Coast for their knowledge, innovative techniques, and integrity. The wooden ships built at Grays Harbor by such well-known builders as Thomas Mac-Donald, Peter and Gordon Frazier Matthews, John Lindstrom, George Hitchings and his Nova Scotia-born partner, John Joyce, were in steady demand. If building ships was no problem in Aberdeen, financing them could be, even though the price of a finished ship was not then great by today's values. New ships were not always able to find backers, and speculating on their sale once they were completed could be risky. When they were not built to order, a popular method on the harbor of financing them was primitive, communal, and effective, becoming by mutual investment a local project: the town bankers, sawmill owners, well-to-do merchants, assorted local investors, and often the captain-to-be of the new vessel would each purchase shares in the ship to spread the cost of her construction. It was a method that worked very well.

As there were shipbuilders on Grays Harbor, so were there sailors and captains to sail the ships built there. Seamen came to the harbor towns looking for berths, knowing that wherever ships were built and loaded, crews were needed to sail them. Many seamen, unlettered and often living hard lives, found their immigrant neighbors at Grays Harbor familiar and comfortable. The townspeople, most of them mill hands, farmers, fishermen, merchants, and assorted workmen, offered open-handed welcome to the seafaring men; they were recognized as their own kind, men they were able to understand easily and quickly. These uneducated sailors, cosmopolitans of the world's seaports, brought their rugged virtues to Grays Harbor, where they were received with pleasure.

The ships at Grays Harbor, the pride of the West Coast shipping community, were a heartening sight. Apart from their trim beauty, loaded ships meant profitable business, the very success symbols that Grays Harbor's citizens sought eagerly. Deeply loaded with fresh-sawn lumber in their cavernous holds, the ships took on deckloads as well, which often towered as much as fourteen feet higher than the main decks. Unbarked trees sixty to eighty feet long, sold to the trade as pilings, were often threaded through loading ports, large openings cut into the wooden hulls at the ship's bow and stern to facilitate their entry and discharge.

The ships lay alongside one another in tiers at the loading docks, each awaiting its turn to be stowed with lumber by longshoremen expert in the art of loading lumber ships. This almost black art was a crucial one for sailors; it was well known that ships stowed improperly could mean the difference between life and death at sea. For this reason few men were more greatly valued on the mill docks then the stevedore boss. What he knew through long experience about ship stowage was indispensable to men carrying cargoes in sailing vessels. An extra fifty dollars placed in his willing hand was always a sound investment. The loss of a poorly loaded vessel and her crew at sea was neither overlooked nor lightly forgiven by the shipping community.

Once the ship was properly loaded and everything movable secured, the lumber cargo in the hold tightly wedged into place, the deckload chained and turnbuckled so it could not shift under way at sea, then the local tugboatman took center stage, for now the heavy ship required careful handling, and no one undervalued the tugboatman's unique ability to handle such vessels skillfully. It was his stock in trade, and he had to be good at it for he was rarely given a second chance to fail badly. The loaded ship, an intractable, near-inert mass of many tons, had first to be unmoored from its dock, carefully snaked down one of the harbor's narrow rivers, through slowly opening swing bridges, towed free and clear of other ships lining both banks and finally out of the river and into the broad Chehalis, westbound, downstream to the ocean.

It was not alone for their dependable steam power and maneuverability that tugboats were needed at Grays Harbor. Everyone understood that it was the knowledge the tobacco-chewing tugboat skippers had in their heads about the shifting sandbars in the river and at the sea entrance that made them invaluable. In their persons was embodied the much-needed local pilot. On Grays Harbor the river pilots and the bar pilots were both absolute necessities, a fact of life it took some ship owners and some cost-saving shipmasters a while to accept. Even though the way downriver might look simple to a landlubber, the multichanneled route to the sea was far more dangerous than it appeared. Not only were there sandbars, strong currents, and tricky eddies to watch out for, but the muddy foreshore had to be avoided, since the navigable channels changed shape and position each day. It was no place for an amateur to be towing loaded ships. There were always other dangers. The river could be full of snags, floating refuse great and small from the sawmills, that could easily punch a hole in a wooden ship's hull. These snags, gnarled and twisted roots, were sometimes floating free and could be seen and avoided, while others, no less dangerous, lay submerged, caught in the mud on the river's bottom.

Then too, small fishing boats in the river, often no more than a blurred spot rising and falling in a running sea, were difficult to see in time and could easily be run down. The little river steamers, called "stinkpots" by old-timers, presented other problems in the busy river, especially when rain fell heavily. And finally there was fog, thick, blinding, and long-lasting. Although the river was a godsend to all in a hundred ways, it could become a formidable enemy in one tragic instant. Under all these conditions, the red and green running lights and the belching smokestack of the tug, bobbing up and down at the towing end of a long hawser up ahead, gave comfort to anxious seamen on the long tow downriver.

Although each pioneer settler had rowed, paddled, and sailed his boat up and down the river, it was quickly found that the riverboats, no more than tiny steam-powered vessels when they finally came, served the fledgling communities best. Anything that moved dependably in water was acceptable; stern-wheelers, side-wheelers, and simple propeller-driven steamers.

Each one filled a community need, and they never seemed to be idle, puffing and panting almost every day from Westport on the south shore at the harbor's mouth to the head of the harbor, sixteen miles to the east, and thence further eastward up the narrowed Chehalis to Montesano. They stopped at each of the harbor towns on the way up the river—in earlier times at the command of any passenger. They transported goods and people and, when required, balky and bellowing livestock as well.

Pressed into daily uses required by the townsfolk, the tiny steamers met all needs, taking families on picnics to the ocean beaches, carrying goods to and from the various harbor towns, towing loaded vessels to the sea when the tugboats were busy elsewhere, and, decked out with black crepe, doubling as solemn hearses for the dead, carrying them to upriver cemeteries for burial. The land was not so marshy upriver, and it was universally agreed that the departed should be buried where the incoming tide might not wash them away. Sometimes the tiny steamers provided no more than a commuter ferry service, a mere "spit and a holler" trip across the Wishkah or the Hoquiam. After bridges were built across them, the little steamboats found other useful work. The beloved little vessels were dear to every citizen of the harbor in some small way or another, and the familiar shriek of their whistles, the plumed smoke from their exhausting engines signaling their comings and goings, was reassuring to all. Although tiny and a bit underpowered, the steamers were stout ships, and they served the tidewater towns on the harbor honorably and long.

It was impossible to live in Grays Harbor and ignore the lumber ships that filled its busy rivers. The docks bordering the sawmills that lined the river were shouldered day in and day out with waiting vessels, tiers of them, each settling deeper into the water as heavy cargoes of lumber were loaded into their yawning holds. On days that were heavy with rain-swollen clouds, the scene was gray and dismal. That was most of the time, for good weather was rare on the harbor. Mud seemed everywhere always, and whatever was damp glistened with a dull wet luster. Infrequently dry days at the harbor were eagerly used to dry sails that always seemed to be damp; wet sails were a nuisance. They dripped water endlessly, and sailors knew that unless they were dried at every opportunity, mildew would inevitably rot them at the seams. The dark, wetted sails were a sight to remember as they dried, whitening in the wind. They tugged at their hanks and hoops, crackling and snapping at every gust in apparent ecstasy at their transformation.

Ships were handsome then, white-winged beauties all. Slipping at their moorings and tugging noisily on their lines, they each curtsied and pawed at the water as though angered at the bonds restraining them. Grays Harbor was a proper sailor's delight, where every type of ship was on display—two-, three-, four-, and five-masted schooners, powerful skys'l yard barkentines, tired and worn brigantines, and useful but ungainly wooden steam schooners. They included lumber carriers well known and much admired on the Coast, square riggers hailing from European ports, stately Downeasters hauling lumber in their weary old age, and massive four-mast barks, foreigners, fresh up from South America's West Coast bound for European ports with Grays Harbor's best Douglas fir.

Sea gulls wheeled overhead noisily like tumbling cartwheels in the sky as ship's gear cracked and strained in the strong wind. Mill whistles added their hoarse counterpoint under heavy skies, and the many sounds of commerce, of ships and men afloat and under way, lent life where otherwise at Grays Harbor there was only the natural grandeur of the sea, the sky, and the forests.

In the quiet Wishkah, refuse from the sawmills lining its banks, the waiting vessels make a handsome picture, under the brooding shadow of East Aberdeen's "Think of Me" Hill, a reminder to seafaring men of the local cigar of the same name. The three-mast schooner Comet built in 1886 by the Hall Brothers at Port Blakeley, the steam schooner Centralia, a 1902 product of John Dickie's San Francisco yards, and other ships at the mill docks await their cargoes.

Waiting for lumber to be sawn and loaded seemed endless at busy Grays Harbor mills. The barkentine Arago, built in Bend, Oregon, in 1891, and other vessels, moored outboard of one another, sailing ship and steamer alike, bob and tug on their lines. Loading could take three weeks and longer; the time dragged.

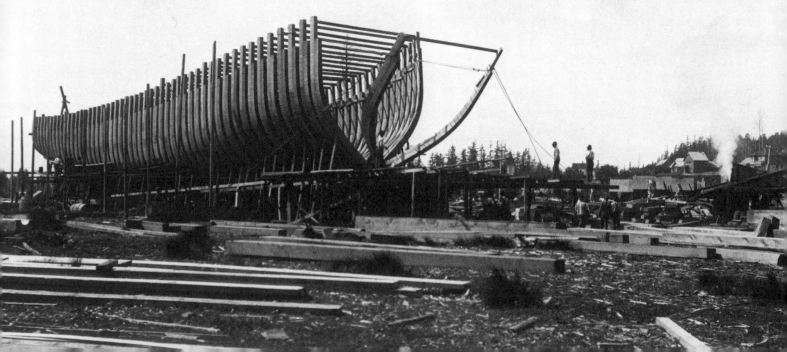

Opposite top: *Ships to carry lumber were badly needed in 1897, and the shipyards on the harbor did their best to provide them. Here the midship frames, great balks of timber bolted together, are being erected on the building schooner's keel. When completed, the entire assemblage forms the vessel's skeleton.*

Opposite bottom: *Raising frames at the forming bow is a careful piece of work. Block and tackle, brains and brawn do the trick. Knowledge perfected by generations of able shipbuilders helps these Aberdeen craftsmen fasten each timber in its proper place securely, the only guarantee of a stout vessel.*

The framed-in hull is nearly completed at last. Though the stem and stern are not yet finished, even a landlubber can quickly recognize the familiar form. The long horizontal timbers along the outside of the frames, the ribbands, will guide the plankers when they commence their work.

Opposite top: *Two sailing schooners, perhaps the Eldorado in 1901 and the Watson A. West, early in 1902, rise on their building ways in Bill Mc-Whinney's yard between the West and Slade mills in East Aberdeen. The nearer is largely planked, the farther vessel still being framed. The low-roofed shed at right houses the band-saw, providing the complex sawn timbers needed at every step in the construction of a wooden ship.*

Opposite bottom: *Captain J. J. Weatherwax, an early sawmill owner, launched this 384-ton three-mast schooner, named for himself, in Aberdeen in 1890. The launching, a gala civic event, was attended by almost everyone in Aberdeen. Captain Weatherwax, his friends, and his fellow investors all regarded the newly built schooner as a certain omen for the continued success of the Weatherwax mill.*

The four-mast schooner Kailua, built by Hitchings and Joyce at Hoquiam in 1901 for Hind, Rolph and Company, is but minutes away from her successful launch. Each onlooker has a stake in the vessel's future, and their interest is understandably high. As Grays Harbor–built ships make profitable voyages, the townspeople investing in them expect to share in the resulting good fortune.

Opposite: *A typical town project involving small investors, the four-mast schooner Defiance, built by Peter Matthews for the E. K. Wood Lumber Company, sits on her launching ways in 1897 ready to slide into the Hoquiam River. Her four lower masts are seated in their mast steps, an American flag flies at her jigger pole, and each stick of cargo she will load bears the financial aspirations of the tiny community.*

The new four-mast schooner Melrose, built by Hitchings and Joyce in 1902 at their Hoquiam yard, is a home product in its entirety. The lumber to build her came from local forests and was sawn to size in local mills, and local artisans completed her construction. Here she is towed down the Hoquiam River on her maiden voyage, her fourteen-foot deckload of Grays Harbor prime fir the object of scrutiny by professional log-boom tenders on the shore.

Twice Mayor of Aberdeen, president of his own shipbuilding company, and a highly skilled craftsman, John Lindstrom built many vessels for Pacific Coast shipowners at his Aberdeen yard. Three steam schooners in different stages of completion are shown building under sheds to protect them and the workmen from the incessant Grays Harbor wetness.

Crowded with company officials, the owner's invited guests, and assorted well-wishers, another Lindstrom-built vessel, a single-ended steam schooner, slides into the Chehalis. Her newly painted hull gleaming in the afternoon sun, flags flying, her entrance is fittingly grand.

Opposite: Two local brass bands stand ready to usher the completed stern-wheel steamer Montesano down her greased ways into the muddy Chehalis. Built by the Grays Harbor Commercial Company at Cosmopolis in 1889, she replaced an earlier, slower steamer of the same name imported into the harbor from Astoria, Oregon. The new stern-wheeler became famous for her fast, dependable service from Montesano, her home port, downriver to the ocean beaches.

Stacked high with a deckload of the same kind of lumber used to build her, the steam schooner Dirigo minus her engines leaves the Peter Matthews yard in Hoquiam, her launching site in 1898. The snow is still on the raw hills, the wind brisk, and her crew gives thanks for the sails forward to help steady her on the long tow south to San Francisco. There at the Union Engine Works she will have her engines installed.

Fresh out of her building yard in 1888, the tiny steam schooner Point Loma, one of the early examples of her breed, passes down the Hoquiam River. The builders of the earliest steam schooners incorporated many features of sailing ships in the design and construction. Seafaring men, traditionally conservative, were frequently unwilling to give new notions their quick approval, and only by relying on familiar features could the hard heads and diehards among them be reassured.

In the shadow of East Aberdeen's familiar hills, lying at the Slade mill dock in the Wishkah in 1908, one of John Dickie's San Francisco–built single-enders, the saucy Newburg, and her two companions load sawn lumber for shipment south. After their holds are filled, topped off, and wedged into place, their empty decks are piled with more lumber, chained and wedged to keep it from shifting on the rough voyage down the Pacific Coast.

Loading cargo at the Hoquiam Lumber Company, not far from where Hitchings and Joyce built her in 1902, the four-mast schooner Melrose and her consort at the mill dock, the Bendixsen schooner Allen A., built in Fairhaven in 1888, lend color and life to this Hoquiam River scene on an otherwise typical, gray working day in 1906.

Opposite: The lofty barkentine Newsboy at right, the white-painted schooner W. J. Patterson at left, and the steam schooner Harold Dollar, pictured loading Grays Harbor lumber at the Hoquiam mills, form a graceful sea picture. The solitary seafarer rowing his heavy Columbia River salmon boat in midstream provides the human touch this vivid image requires.

Below: *As lumber was loaded round the clock at Grays Harbor, the sweet-smelling sawmill docks were rarely empty of ships. Two tiers of vessels jostling each other side by side in the crowded dock sink deeper, down to their marks, as sling load after sling load of mill-sawn lumber is stowed in their yawning holds.*

Opposite: *Schooners line up for their cargoes from the A. J. West mill dock in Aberdeen as elephants do in a circus parade. At left, the white-painted W. J. Patterson, Aberdeen's pride; astern of her the handsome four-masted Forester, built in 1900 by Hay and Wright at their Alameda yard. Further astern lies the four-mast schooner A. J. West, a namesake of the pioneer Aberdeen sawmill operator.*

Opposite: *Aberdeen at its most typical, mill docks bustling with activity, the overcast skies filled with steam, smoke, and the hoarse cries of hard-working men. At the Slade mill dock the steam schooner Newburg tops off a staggering deckload and fills her fresh-water tanks from the water barge alongside. Astern of her the newly arrived*

four-mast schooner F. M. Slade, built for the Slade Mill by Mc-Whinney and Cousins at their Aberdeen yard in 1900, towers over the scene, dwarfing everything else by comparison.

Below: *However it was done, loading lumber on ships paid the bills. Every loaded steam schooner could mean a profit, and nothing interfered, not even the weather. On a typical muddy day when all of Grays Harbor seems wet and gray, the steam schooners Santa Barbara and Santa Monica, veterans of the Pacific Coast's "Scandinavian Navy," take on their dripping cargo at an Aberdeen mill dock.*

Below: *What seems to be random and disorderly in this view on the deck of a steam schooner loading lumber at Grays Harbor is but an instant in a well-organized plan to make up a load safe for transit by sea. Stowing various lengths and sizes of lumber in an orderly fashion, creating a compact mass that can be chained so it is immovable, is work for skilled men. Building such deckloads was a high art, greatly relied on by seamen who trusted their ships and their lives to experienced Grays Harbor stevedores.*

Opposite: *The steam schooner Claremont, a 1907 product of John Lindstrom's Aberdeen yard, offers convincing evidence of the staggering amount of lumber carried in a deckload. It is high proof of the stevedore's skill who stowed it and a tribute to the shipmaster who would put to sea with it. The final test would be out in the boisterous Pacific, bound south in the teeth of a bucking gale.*

Sturdy and stubborn, impressive in her seagoing power, the tug Astoria, built in North Bend, Oregon, in 1884, makes her slow way downriver at Hoquiam, a picture of chilly grace.

The Hoquiam towboat Printer *built locally in 1889 sits quietly in the Hoquiam River.*

This photograph provides ample demonstration of the critical need for steam tugs on Grays Harbor. Carefully towing a loaded three-mast schooner down the narrow Wishkah River, through the opened swing bridge, the tug squeezes by the three-mast schooner *Orient* and the barkentine *Wrestler*, an old-timer built by the Hall Bros. at Port Blakely in Washington Territory in 1880.

When the Wishkah docks were crowded, the close quarters were always risky, particularly for a stubborn skipper determined not to hire a steam tug to tow his vessel clear. Threading her way through the narrow channel, downriver, the heavily loaded steam schooner Santa Monica scrapes past the newly arrived four-mast schooner Edward R. West at right and the three-mast Charles E. Falk at left.

With steam up and ready to go, the tugs Traveler and John Cudahy wait impatiently in the Hoquiam River for the call that will put them to work towing logs to the mill or ships to sea.

Calm in their acknowledged competence, the crew of the Hoquiam tug Traveler, *each man a tough, experienced tug-boater, sit for a group portrait at their tug's stern.*

Below: *Behind the slowly lift-ing fogs, sailing ships and steamers waited impatiently. The white-painted steamer Cosmopolis, loaded to her marks, frets on her lines while next to her the aging brigan-tine, T. W. Lucas, built way back in 1857 at Bath, Maine, idles at her moorings, waiting, waiting....*

Opposite: *Another ancient craft, the weary little brigan-tine W. H. Meyer, built in 1869 at San Francisco as a two-mast schooner, here seen towing down the Hoquiam River, remained in service only so long as her equally tired crews could man her pumps to keep her afloat.*

An early view of the Wishkah River some time after 1892 when the three-mast schooner at the mill dock at left, the O. M. Kellog, was built by Hans Bendixsen at Fairhaven, California. Gently listing at her dock at right, the stern-wheeler Montesano prepares to depart for the ocean beaches, while in the stream a rare old-timer, an uncommon rig on the Pacific Coast, the topsail schooner Monitor, built in 1862, warps into her berth.

Three early lumber droghers—two firewood schooners and a barkentine, all tiny carriers—wait for their cargoes at A. J. West's sawmill in the Wishkah at Aberdeen, 1889. It is only four lonely years since the small mill began cutting its first timber, the same four years since Aberdeen was formally organized as a town.

There was always seagoing beauty somewhere on Grays Harbor. This is a view in the Wishkah River of the three-mast schooner Occidental drying sails in good weather, the brigantine Geneva likewise occupied at the West mill dock, and the steamer T. C. Reed preparing to cast off from her Heron and G street dock in Aberdeen.

Named after one of Aberdeen's most successful bankers, a likely shareholder as well, the white-hulled four-mast schooner W. J. Patterson, newly built at John Lindstrom's Aberdeen shipyard in 1901, lies empty at a Hoquiam dock awaiting her first cargo and her maiden voyage.

Opposite: *Built up north at Sea-beck, Washington, on Puget Sound in 1881, the barkentine Mary Winkleman dries her sails at the Slade Mill wharf in Aberdeen. Deeper into the narrow Wishkah, the barken-tine Newsboy, built in 1882 at San Francisco by John Dickie, and the three-mast schooner Comet finish loading for their southbound passage.*

Below: *Although it is the Hoquiam River, the scene could be anywhere on Grays Harbor. Low hills like this, with some trees still standing and other sections cut over, slashed, and burned, are typical. The newly built local tugboat Astoria tows the Esther Buhne, a loaded* three-mast schooner from *Eureka, California, downriver to the sea. The only untypical note is the welcome sunshine —a bonus any day on Grays Harbor.*

Hoquiam at its most typical. Shadowing the dense timber stands, leaden skies burden the horizon. Newly cleared land, dotted with fresh construction, gapes as though it is a new wound in the earth. Hoquiam's earliest steam schooner, Cosmopolis, built in 1887 to inaugurate service between San Francisco and Grays Harbor, snakes her way to an upriver sawmill for her cargo.